CAUGHT UNAWARE

Dud. Spark but no fire. Just like that ruse with the slaughtered horses.

"Damn," he muttered and struck another. This time the lucifer caught and he lit the quirlie. He took a deep drag, then said, "What you doin', hidin' in the shadows, Marcus?"

"Mighty brave, don't you think?" Marcus moved into the moonlight, hand on his gun.

Slocum froze. "What do you mean?"

"For a man who nearly got his head blowed off this afternoon. Steppin' out, striking a match in the dark, no gun. Purty easy target, if someone wanted to take potshots . . . and how'd you know it was me?"

"Smelled your stink, polecat, and I don't need a gun for no varmint—"

Behind him, the screen door banged. Then he saw the glint of cold steel emerging from near his side and heard the ratchet of a hammer being cocked . . .

JAKE LOGAN

SLOCUM
AND THE
HORSE KILLERS

J

JOVE BOOKS, NEW YORK

THE BERKLEY PUBLISHING GROUP
Published by the Penguin Group
Penguin Group (USA) Inc.
375 Hudson Street, New York, New York 10014, USA
Penguin Group (Canada), 90 Eglinton Avenue East, Suite 700, Toronto, Ontario M4P 2Y3, Canada
(a division of Pearson Penguin Canada Inc.)
Penguin Books Ltd., 80 Strand, London WC2R 0RL, England
Penguin Group Ireland, 25 St. Stephen's Green, Dublin 2, Ireland (a division of Penguin Books Ltd.)
Penguin Group (Australia), 250 Camberwell Road, Camberwell, Victoria 3124, Australia
(a division of Pearson Australia Group Pty. Ltd.)
Penguin Books India Pvt. Ltd., 11 Community Centre, Panchsheel Park, New Delhi—110 017, India
Penguin Group (NZ), Cnr. Airborne and Rosedale Roads, Albany, Auckland 1310, New Zealand
(a division of Pearson New Zealand Ltd.)
Penguin Books (South Africa) (Pty.) Ltd., 24 Sturdee Avenue, Rosebank, Johannesburg 2196,
South Africa

Penguin Books Ltd., Registered Offices: 80 Strand, London WC2R 0RL, England

This is a work of fiction. Names, characters, places, and incidents either are the product of the author's imagination or are used fictitiously, and any resemblance to actual persons, living or dead, business establishments, events, or locales is entirely coincidental.

SLOCUM AND THE HORSE KILLERS

A Jove Book / published by arrangement with the author

PRINTING HISTORY
Jove edition / July 2006

Copyright © 2006 by The Berkley Publishing Group.

ISBN: 0-515-14046-5

JOVE®
Jove Books are published by The Berkley Publishing Group,
a division of Penguin Group (USA) Inc.,
375 Hudson Street, New York, New York 10014.
JOVE is a registered trademark of Penguin Group (USA) Inc.
The "J" design is a trademark belonging to Penguin Group (USA) Inc.

PRINTED IN THE UNITED STATES OF AMERICA

10 9 8 7 6 5 4 3 2 1

1

Slocum, fresh from the trail and relaxing in Monkey Springs's Prairie Hen Saloon, sat quickly forward in his chair, dropping the legs to the floor with a loud bang. "What the hell did you say?" he asked the surprised bartender.

"I s-said there's a gent out in the street," the barkeep mumbled apologetically. "Said he's callin' you out. Are you really him, mister? Are you really *the* Slocum? The one they write about?"

Slocum's face twisted with annoyance. "Yeah," he muttered. "Who's out there? You know?"

The bartender shrugged and pulled a battered dime novel from his back pocket.

"Can I have your autograph, Mr. Slocum?" he asked, offering it. It was *Slocum and the Badlands Bullies,* and the horse he was riding on the cover was a pinto. He'd never ridden a pinto in his life.

"No," said Slocum, scraping back his chair as he stood. Why did these lunatics follow him around?

Back in Tucson, there'd been a wet-behind-the-ears kid

wanting to fan his reputation, too. Slocum had lost him by running out the back door, and the kid hadn't tracked him down again.

Just lucky that time, he reckoned.

But this saloon didn't have a back door. He supposed he'd have to kill somebody again, and for no reason.

Or maybe, just maybe, he could talk his way out of it.

He supposed he'd have to talk directly to the fellow calling him out, though. And stalling would only make the son of a bitch more obstinate.

Slocum crossed the room—the few men behind him in the bar eager for a show but keeping their distance—and pushed through the batwing doors. He looked both ways, up and down the newly deserted street, which had been thick with carts and horses and people when he first rode down it.

He spotted his challenger, about a block away to the west. Standing smack in front of the afternoon sun.

It figured.

He stepped down off the walk and into the street. There wasn't another human being on it besides himself and the man who'd challenged him. There was no other living thing, other than a cur bitch lying on the sidewalk, which some unseen woman was desperately trying to coax into a doorway.

"Sassy, come!" she whispered in a desperate tenor. "Sassy, come here right now!"

Ignoring her entirely, the dog merely rolled onto its back.

The man, a silhouette against the sun, started slowly walking toward Slocum. He couldn't make the man out yet, not in any detail, although he appeared to be of a size with Slocum, which took him out of the callow and heedless youth category.

Slocum squinted while the man peeled off his right glove. Damn, he hated this shit!

The figure neared, then stopped. And stood there, silently. There was no sound at all, except for the whistle of the low wind and that poor woman, still trying to get Sassy to come inside and out of danger.

Slocum grumbled to himself. Why the hell didn't the varmint draw? Or do *something*? Was this fool out to kill him with boredom?

And then the figure spoke.

"You gonna stand there all day, Slocum, or you gonna ask an old buddy to have a drink?"

Slocum frowned. He knew that voice!

"Crone?" he asked incredulously. "Dave Crone?"

The figure lifted a hand and slapped his thigh. "'Bout damn time, Slocum!" he said, between jagged peals of laughter. "I thought for a minute I was actually gonna have to shoot you!"

Slocum grinned. "That'll be the day, Crone. C'mon," he said, waving a hand. "I'll buy you a beer."

Crone cackled again. "Don't mind if I do, Slocum, don't mind at all!"

While Sassy finally got up, shook herself off, and went inside the door across the way, Slocum waited until the figure reached him and stepped out of the sun's glare to assume not only the voice, but the visage of David Erasmus Crone—cowpuncher, range rider, pretty fair tracker, former Pinkerton man, and now, retired counter man.

At least, Slocum figured he had quit ringing the money up at that Taos gunsmith's shop. New Mexico was a long way from Monkey Springs in the Arizona Territory.

Crone made himself at home at Slocum's table, and Slocum called for a couple of fresh beers.

"Real funny, Crone," he said, picking up his beer. "Callin' me out like that. Don't you know you almost got yourself killed, putting yourself between me and the sun?"

Crone, a good-sized man with short, grizzled, dark brown hair and a thick mustache to match, replied, "Can't say that I wasn't tryin' to, Slocum." He twirled his beer mug with an idle finger. "Then again, didn't figure you to actually draw until you was drawn on."

Slocum sat back and took a thoughtful sip. "Got a point," he said. "But damn, Crone! What you doin' out in this neck of the woods, anyhow? You give up watchin' the cashbox at Morton's Gunsmith Shop?"

Crone nodded a quick yes. "Borin', Slocum. Terrible borin'. Worse'n watchin' cactus grow. And then, two weeks ago, I got me a reprieve."

Slocum cocked a brow. "And that was?"

Crone leaned over the table on his elbows and grinned. "You remember Vance Jefferson?"

Slocum certainly did. Who could forget Jefferson's lone charge on the Downy boys, over at Foxtail Canyon, or the way he'd handled that deal with Ferris Heron, over on the Colorado River?

A few other celebrated events had been attributed to Vance Jefferson, too, but Slocum had been around for both the Downy boys and Ferris's last stand, so he only counted those two as real. He knew how tongues wagged, and the ways of reporters and dime novelists, eager for a good tall story.

He nodded and just said, "Yup."

Crone's head nodded. "Well, I heared he's dead. Heared he got hisself kilt. And over a dance-hall girl! Ain't that somethin'?"

Slocum furrowed his brow. He couldn't figure out why

Crone seemed so damned happy about it. Jefferson had saved Crone's gizzard once or twice, after all.

But then Crone added, "Bob Marcus done it. I'm goin' up there to find him and settle the score."

"Seems to me that it'd take more'n Bob Marcus to take down Jefferson, Crone," Slocum said quietly. "Not that I mean to doubt your word."

"Oh, understood, Slocum!" Crone said, and polished off his beer. He called to the barkeep for another, then added, "Slocum, they say that Granger Foley was with him. Do you know Foley?"

"Mostly by reputation," Slocum said. "Heard he killed Tom Villard over cards."

Crone nodded. "He sure did. He shot him over my way, in New Mexico Territory. Marcus, I mean; Marcus shot Jefferson. He's a mean piece'a business, and he's hooked up with Foley now. The Lord knows why."

He stood up, met the bartender halfway to the table, and brought back his full mug.

"And you're gonna go and avenge Vance Jefferson, all by your lonesome?" Slocum asked. He hadn't even put a dent in his beer yet. He picked it up and took a gulp, if only in the interest of keeping things closer to even.

"Yes, I am, by God!" announced Crone. "Ol' Jefferson, he picked me up from a dry wady at a full gallop back in '77, saved my bacon from the bunch of them scum-suckers that Juan Alba calls his gang. A man don't forget somethin' like that, no sir!"

Crone must have dome something pretty rank to piss off Juan Alba's boys, Slocum thought, but said nothing. He sucked on his beer.

"Well, Crone, I wish you luck."

Crone's face wadded up a mite. "What?"

"I said, best of luck to you."

Crone brought his beer mug down hard, sloshing foam over his hand. "Dad gum it! You're supposed to come with me! Ain't that the way this works?"

Slocum studied on this for a moment, then said, with a straight face, "The way what works, Crone? Don't believe I follow you."

A look of disgust crossed Crone's face, followed by one of abject disappointment. "I'm supposed to tell you what happened to ol' Vance—and who done it—and you're supposed to whatchacall . . . jump on the vengeance bandwagon with me!"

Slocum nodded. "Got you, Crone. But y'see, I'm expected in Apache Wells. And that's where I'm goin'."

Crone's face lit up. "Well, that's fine, just fine! Marcus and Foley was last seen riding that away!"

Slocum groaned.

2

The next day found Slocum riding alongside a jabbering Dave Crone as the two made their way toward Apache Wells.

Slocum had tried his best to avoid having company—by getting Crone as drunk as possible the night before, and by sneaking down to the livery at 5:00 am—but it seemed fate had stuck him with Crone, for good or for ill.

Crone had been standing outside the stable, sober as a judge, waiting for him, and making a show of checking his watch.

Dave Crone was harder to get rid of than a case of the smallpox.

And talk? If it wasn't this, it was that, and then the other thing. No subject was too boring to keep him from orating for a minimum of a half hour.

He did forty-five minutes on the origin of his goddamn shirt buttons, then another hour on the superiority of ivory to bone!

Lucky for Slocum that Crone didn't expect him to keep

up the other end of the conversation. Crone must have seen himself as an all-knowing lecturer, pure and simple. Which allowed Slocum to just ride and let Crone's words turn into a hum. An annoying hum, to be sure, but a hum none the less.

Now Slocum understood why Crone had enjoyed such a short career with the Pinkertons. He had probably talked them to death.

Slocum figured it would take them until just after dark to make Apache Wells, and he was pretty sure they wouldn't find Bob Marcus or Granger Foley anywhere near it. Despite a couple of months with the Pinkertons, Crone never had much of a nose for finding fellows.

Now, what Slocum was hoping for was a little different—to find Miss Miranda Cassidy in a fine fettle and waiting with open arms.

And legs.

Not that he didn't care about Vance Jefferson. Jefferson had been a good pal to him, way back when. And if Slocum should happen to run across his killers, he supposed he'd take care of them. Quickly, and in a way they wouldn't like.

In ol' Jefferson's name, of course.

But his blood was running too hot at the moment to think about anything except Miranda.

She'd wired him, all the way down in Mexico City.

Just how she'd tracked him down was anybody's guess, but she'd said there was some trouble with her uncle's ranch. It was probably the next thing to nothing, but Slocum had dropped everything—including the señorita he'd been with at the time—to ride north. Miranda was that special.

Her uncle owned the Bar C (and her father before him),

and he raised some of the finest quarter-mile running horses in the Territory. He'd offered Slocum a nice mare the last time he'd been through Apache Wells, but Slocum wouldn't ride anything but an Appaloosa.

He was, in fact, still riding the same horse he'd been on for a year—Cougar, a glowing red dun with a snowflake blanket. Cougar was steady on the rein, didn't have a spooky bone in his body, and was soft-mouthed. Slocum liked him fine.

And as he remembered, Miss Miranda was pretty soft-mouthed, too.

Soft everywhere. Big, pillowy breasts, a nipped-in waist, belled hips, long legs, and a real attitude. What more could a man ask for?

"What you grinnin' about?" Crone asked, right in the middle of all that incessant babble.

Slocum twisted slowly toward him, his saddle creaking slightly. "What?"

"I said, what you grinnin' about, dad gum it!" Crone demanded testily. "Here I'm tellin' you all the terrible things them Yaquis can do to a man, and there you sit with a smile splittin' your face! Calhoun Taylor gettin' his hide peeled off by a band of grinnin' heathen ain't my definition of a laughin' matter!"

"Sorry, Crone," Slocum said, doing his best to keep a straight face. He didn't remember anything about any Yaquis or Calhoun Taylor, and was sort of pleased that he'd missed it. "Woolgatherin', I reckon."

Crone nodded. "I suppose you was thinkin' 'bout what you're gonna do to Marcus and Foley when we catch up to 'em. Well, hell, that'd put a grin on my face, too! What you got planned, Slocum?" He lowered his voice to a whisper. "Is it terrible cunning?"

"No, Crone," Slocum said, and squeezed Cougar with his knees, urging him into a trot. "Just thinkin' that the bar in Apache Wells keeps more variety on tap than that hole back in Monkey Springs did, that's all. Thinkin' about havin' me some fine champagne."

Crone cackled wildly while trying to keep his seat. He was riding a stout bay with short legs, and the horse could barely keep up with Slocum's rangy Cougar. This was not lost on Slocum, who pushed Cougar to move a little faster.

"Say-ay-ay, Slocum-um," called Crone, whose mount was currently doing something resembling a Missouri Fox Trot, only less smooth. "Slow-ow-ow down-wn-wn!"

With a snort, Slocum reined Cougar down to a shambling walk. "Sorry," he said. "But we've got to make better time if we want to make Apache Wells by sundown."

"Well, we ain't goin' nowhere at this blood-blisterin' trot!" Dave complained as he caught up. "My backside'll be beat to a bloody pulp inside a mile! Why you gotta ride them speckled giraffes, anyways?"

Crone stopped grumbling long enough to satisfy an itch at the back of his neck, then added, "Now, iffen you was to do a slow lope on that critter, I reckon me and Tommy could keep up with you if we was to gallop full out." He paused. "Just not for very long, understand? Tommy's got a lot of bottom, but I ain't gonna kill him just so's you can have a drink!"

Eager to escape another lecture on saddle-making, the intrinsic superiority of ivory, or the art of cooking beets, Slocum nodded and clucked to Cougar, putting him into an easy lope.

The stocky Tommy followed behind, legs pumping to beat the band while Crone fanned his backside.

•   •   •

Slocum had no more than tied his horse at the rail outside McGuffy's Hotel and Saloon than he heard a ruckus coming his way. He had half-turned toward the voices when a hand on his back stopped him, then shoved him, face-first, into the water trough!

Sputtering and swearing, he pulled himself up by the edge while Crone laughed and slapped his thighs.

Slocum stood, hands balled into fists, and wheeled about, his fists cocked, while spattering and scattering droplets like a retriever fresh from the river. He pulled his punch about a half inch from a pretty female face atop a knockout figure that was barely more than five feet tall.

"Miranda Cassidy?" he said in shock and surprise. "What the hell are you—?"

A big lump of a galoot in a checkered shirt pushed her protectively out of the way, right into Crone's arms. "Who're you?" he demanded. "What call do you got to butt in?"

Crone, putting Miranda aside, said, "Are you crazy, boy? That's Slocum! *The* Slocum, his own dang self!"

Immediately, the man took a step back, and for once, Slocum was glad that somebody had called attention to those damned dime books. He wasn't much in the frame of mind to take on this big bull.

The bull's eyebrows worked for a while before he asked, "Is that right? Are you really Slocum? I thought he was made up!"

"Of course he's real, Berto!" cried Miranda, pushing her way forward. She wrapped her arms around Slocum's damp waist and said, "I told you he'd come, didn't I?"

"Yeah, but I thought you was teasin' me again, Miss Miranda," muttered Berto the bull.

She looked longingly up at Slocum, and all of a sudden, his britches felt a couple of sizes too small.

Which she noticed, because she looked down, then looked up again with a peculiar grin on her face.

Slocum remembered that grin.

"Nice to see you, too," she said slyly.

"You're an ornery little minx, Miranda," he quipped. "And you're gonna be soaked through pretty soon, too," he added, squeezing water from his sleeve. "Among other things."

He pried her off him so that he could take her arm, and led her into the hotel, which just happened to be the saloon, as well.

"So tell me, sweetheart," he said as he pushed open the batwing doors. "What exactly has got your knickers in such a knot, and how in hell did you ever track me down?"

"You remember Carmelita?"

"Sure!" She was the best damned cook in the county, and had been out at the Bar C since Miranda's mother was alive.

"Well, it seems she can work wonders with things besides fried catfish and cherry cobbler."

"Just as long as she doesn't go hangin' one of those charm jiggers on my door again. I don't go for gettin' hit in the face by a dead rooster's feet first thing in the mornin'."

Miranda patted his arm. "Now, now. She's gotten over that."

3

"Come and sit down, and I'll tell you about the ranch," Miranda said, looking for all the world like she wasn't about to tell him a dang blasted thing until she got what she wanted.

Which, knowing Miranda, he suspected was exactly what she had in mind for him, too.

That suited him just fine.

Laughing, she lifted a coy, finely arched brow, and then ran a hand down his arm. "Something to rinse your pipes, now you've had a nice, refreshing bath?" Her hand roved to his leg like she planned on taking up ownership. She softly stroked the hard muscles of his thigh.

At this rate, he'd never dry off. She had him steamed up and sweating like a racehorse!

Before Slocum could open his mouth to answer, she had dragged him through the saloon's door to a table, and held up two fingers to the barkeep. A dripping glass for each of them appeared on the scarred bar.

Miranda hopped up and sauntered over to retrieve them,

13

red curls trailing over her shoulders, and said in a loud voice, "Mr. Slocum's checking in, Harvey."

Miranda's backside was sleek and round as a Bar C mare, Slocum thought. And the way it jiggled and bounced under her bright calico, it was a sight easier to look at. A damn sight easier.

Suddenly much warmer, Slocum wiped his forehead with the back of a hand. He flicked his eyes toward the door, checking for Crone. He'd taken the horses to the livery, but it was too early for him to be back.

Miranda picked up the drinks and turned toward the table. The left side of her dress was soaked though where she had leaned against him, plastering the wet material to the outline of her body. A dark pink nipple stood up, proudly pointing at him.

Damned if that woman didn't know how to fill out a dress!

Damned if that woman never *could* learn to wear underwear! At least, all the time.

"Drink up," Miranda said as she slid into her chair and handed him a beer. She dropped his room key on the table as she tipped her own drink up and took a long draft, her eyes peering at him over the top of her glass. "Ahhh," she sighed.

The sight of her moist pink tongue slowly licking foam off her top lip nearly made him forget the reason he had let Dave Crone follow along. "So, you goin' to tell me what's been happening at Apache Wells?"

Miranda leaned toward his ear and rested a soft fleshy mound against his forearm. She smiled that peculiar grin of hers again before she answered, "In due time, honey. But not here. Finish your drink. We'll get us a bottle of champagne and go up to your room to talk . . . among other things," Miranda teased, and gave his crotch a smart squeeze.

"What the hell . . . ?" Slocum nearly came out of his chair, but had to admit he liked a woman who showed initiative. "Keep that up, we won't be goin' nowhere any time soon."

Calmly, Miranda removed her hand but arranged her body in a way that gave Slocum full view of her two best features. A slow seductive smile crept over her face, not that he needed more encouragement. Just the memory of those hips grinding figure eights—

"Well if that ain't about as welcome as a skunk in the church aisle!" Slocum heard behind him.

He instantly regretted breaking his own rule: Never sit with your back to the door. With measured slowness, he turned toward the voice. "Bob Marcus. And Granger Foley, I presume. Heard you two were ridin' this way."

Marcus moved a cud of tobacco to his cheek and sent a stream of amber liquid that landed a few inches from Slocum's feet.

Foley's hand inched toward his holster.

Quickly, Marcus placed a hand on Foley's arm and growled an introduction. "Granger Foley, John Slocum."

Foley shrugged him off. "We already met a time or two. Least, almost met up."

"Just what brings you to Apache Wells, Slocum?" Marcus asked, his watery blue eyes darting between Slocum and Miranda.

"Since when does Slocum answer to a couple of trail bums like you two?" Miranda snapped. "Just because Uncle Abel hired you, it doesn't give you the right to interfere in my business."

Hired them? Abel Cassidy had hired Marcus and Foley?

Hell, he could have done better hiring a couple of coyotes to guard the henhouse, Slocum thought.

Slocum was still grinning at the thought of these two spitting feathers when he noticed dried blood splashed on the men's boots and clothing. But before he could give it a second thought, or further ponder the reason Abel Cassidy would engage a couple outlaws, Dave Crone walked up behind Foley and put a hand on his shoulder.

Big mistake.

Faster than a diamondback's strike, Foley whirled around. He caught Crone under his left eye, laying his cheek open to the bone. Foley's next punch caught the burly Crone in the chest, dropping him straight as a lead sinker in a fishing hole. Crone made a loud *ooph* as he hit the floor and kicked up a cloud of sawdust.

Dammit! Slocum thought. In town for less than twenty minutes and already thick into a mess. For someone who rarely started a fight, plenty seemed to find him.

Foley drew his left boot back like he was fixing to kick Crone's teeth in.

Springing to his feet, Slocum grabbed Foley by the shoulder and spun him around.

The rock-hard knuckles of Slocum's right hand landed on Foley's left temple, splitting the skin next to his eye.

Blood spurted from the wound. Now that Slocum had been dragged into it, Foley and Marcus both better count on a good pounding.

He pulled back for another blow.

"That's enough!" Miranda cried.

He froze.

"Marcus! Take Foley back to the ranch," Miranda ordered.

Marcus stepped between Slocum and Foley. Reluctantly, Slocum dropped his arm.

Just dandy. Two new enemies, and here was Miranda taking his back.

Marcus prodded Foley to the bar and ordered whiskey. They quickly tossed their drinks down and headed out the batwing doors. Foley could have frozen a witch's cauldron with the look he shot at Slocum before stepping out to the sidewalk.

Groaning, Crone struggled to his knees. Slocum reached down and hauled him to his feet. Crone pulled a rag from his pants pocket and wiped his face, smearing dirt and blood into a gruesome mask that made the injury appear worse than it was.

And since they had met up at Monkey Springs, it was the first time the blithering idiot was at a loss for words.

"Ain't you got any God-given common sense at all, Crone?" Slocum asked. "You're lucky you didn't catch an extra hole in the head instead of just a cut cheek. Better find the sawbones and let him take a look at it. You might need to get yourself stitched up. I mean, Jesus Christ! What would Alan Pinkerton say?"

"Probably 'Good riddance to bad rubbish,' " muttered Crone. "Least, that's what he said before."

"Down the street to your right, up over Harley Briggs's café," Miranda called to Crone's back.

As Crone staggered out the door, Slocum asked, "Why'd you stop me, Miranda?"

"Grab that bottle of champagne and let's go upstairs," she replied. "I'll tell you everything I know. Which isn't much, I'm afraid."

"And I can help you untie your drawers."

"Oh no, you can't, Mr. Slocum."

Shocked, he asked, "And why not? It's about all I've been thinking of since—"

Miranda grinned and placed her fingers to his lips. "I'm not wearin' any."

Slocum unbuckled his gunbelt and laid it on the nightstand. The springs of the iron bed squeaked as he sprawled on his back. Miranda had hiked her skirts up around her waist and was in the process of rolling a silk stocking down a long shapely leg.

She had indeed not worn drawers.

Slocum stared at the thatch of red curls between her legs and felt himself grow hard. Again. While Miranda removed the other stocking, he worked at the buttons of his shirt.

But when he reached to his pants, she whispered, "Why don't you let me do that?"

Sinuous as a mountain lion on the prowl, Miranda walked to the bed and straddled his legs. "Why have you stayed away from Apache Wells for so long?"

She pulled several tortoiseshell pins from her hair and tossed them next to Slocum's guns. Then she eased her dress off over her head and threw it over the foot of the bed.

"Beats the hell outta me," he replied, rolling a dusky nipple between his fingers.

Miranda moaned softly and shifted her body. "It's been too long, darlin', far too long."

Slocum slid his other hand between her legs and dipped his fingers into her wetness.

Again, Miranda moaned and her eyes glazed slightly. She reached down and rubbed the growing bulge in his pants.

"Gonna tease me all afternoon, darlin'?" Slocum asked

with a slow smile. "Or get down to business?" He pulled Miranda down and found her mouth. Her tongue was the only answer he needed.

Miranda straightened again and opened Slocum's pants, easing them off his hips. Then, smiling that quirky smile of hers, she ran her fingertip around the head of his erect cock.

Slocum grabbed her soft, plump hips and lifted, positioning her to receive his first drive home.

"Oh, yes," she hissed as he entered her. Miranda tightened her knees around his hips and began to rock. "Oh, God, yes."

Plunging into her like an elk in rut, Slocum matched her rhythm. Miranda was a woman who knew when a man wanted to make love, and when he wanted to just plain ease himself. Right now, she was hotter than a Mexican pepper and needed it as badly as he did. Hard and fast. Slocum felt her tighten her internal muscles and knew she was ready.

So was he. More than ready.

The sounds of her squeals and groans of pleasure drove him over the edge. He exploded inside her.

Slowly, his breathing returned to normal.

Tossing her tousled hair over her shoulder, Miranda stood and walked to the washstand. Sweat glistened down her spine and formed droplets at the small of her back. She lifted the pitcher and splashed some water into the basin. Then she wet the corner of a towel and wiped her face, breasts, and stomach.

Slocum rolled a quirlie, stuck it in his mouth, and watched. He flicked the head of a lucifer with his thumbnail and the flame sprang to life.

He held the match to the tip of his smoke and drew several long puffs. *Yep!* he thought. *There's only one thing bet-*

*ter than a good smoke after lovemaking. And that's more
lovin'.*

"What are you grinning at?" Miranda asked as she
turned toward him. "You look sly as a cat that just found
the butter plate. And a bit silly with your pants halfway
down to your knees."

She picked up the bottle of champagne and two water
glasses and returned to the bed.

"Gonna pull them up or take 'em off?" she asked, and
set the bottle and glasses beside the bed.

"That depends entirely on you, darlin'."

Miranda squealed and leapt on top of him, planting a
long wet kiss on his mouth. "In that case . . ." She yanked
his pants off and tossed them to the floor, beside her dress.

"At this rate, I'll never find out why you asked me to
come."

Miranda took on a wicked smile, removed the quirlie
from his hand, and stuck it between her teeth. Drawing a
mouthful of smoke, she blew a row of shaky rings and
handed it back to him.

"I don't recall asking you to," she said. "I think you did
it all on your own." Miranda yelped when Slocum lightly
smacked her backside.

"You know damn well what I mean. What are Bob Marcus and Granger Foley doin' in Apache Wells? Why would
a man like Abel Cassidy do business with a couple of owlhoots like that?"

"Told you, I don't know much," she said. "A few months
back we found a mare back in one of the canyons dead and
butchered. At first, Uncle Abel figured it was the work of a
renegade Apache. They're always busting out of San Car-
los, you know."

"But why'd he think that? Apaches love their horses as

much as their children. They'd never butcher a horse, no matter how hungry they were, except as a last resort. Or if they found it dead, or somethin' . . ."

"Once he came to his senses, Uncle Abel said the same thing." Miranda shivered as though she'd taken a chill. She rubbed her arms briskly.

"Since then," she went on, "we've found more. Seven mares and two stallions and a prime four-year-old gelding—a wonderful roping horse. Couple of this year's foals, too. Who'd want to do such a thing?"

"It don't make sense," Slocum said. "And if it don't make sense, then it ain't true."

"What do you mean?"

"Thieving horses—that I can understand. But just butchering them? That's the part that don't make sense. No, there's more to it . . . and I aim to find out."

4

Slocum rolled out of bed while the sky was still a hazy purple and orange. Miranda purred like a well-contented kitten and stretched before she snuggled into the pillows once again.

Her husky voice stopped him at the door. "Leavin' me again already, darlin'?"

"Just for a little while." Slocum looked over his shoulder. "I ain't leavin' town just yet, honey."

Abruptly, Miranda sat up and the sheet fell to her waist, revealing her ample charms. "I should hope to kiss a pig you're not! Where are you going?"

"Takin' a ride out to the Bar C. Want to take a look around. See if I can figure out what's goin' on out there."

She nodded, red curls spilling over her shoulders. "Grand idea, Slocum."

"In the meantime, just wait for me. I'll be back and we can pick up where we left off last night." He paused, adding, "And keep Crone in town. That fool chatters more than a magpie and makes even less sense. I don't want him talking none."

23

Miranda just laughed. "And you think I could stop him?"

He was glad she found Crone amusing. Slocum found him downright annoying, not to mention pretty damn stupid at times. *But he means well,* he kept reminding himself. Not that it did much good . . .

Apache Wells was quiet as he walked from the hotel to the livery. Cougar poked his head over the stall door and whickered when Slocum entered the barn. The Appaloosa seemed eager to get moving.

Slocum was out of town when the sun broke the horizon, the hot white of day pushing aside the softer, more beautiful colors of dawn. He didn't meet anyone on the road to the Bar C, which suited him just fine.

He wanted to get onto Bar C land without being seen and to take a good gander around the ranch without the interference of anyone, especially a particular pair of Miranda's hired hands.

What had possessed the woman—and her uncle Abel—to keep those two reprobates on the payroll? And what in the hell was up with the blood spattering their boots?

He wasn't a man given to jumping to conclusions, but he'd bet a good saddle they were involved with the slaughter of the horses at the Bar C.

Slocum rolled himself a quirlie and struck a lucifer on the seam of his denims. Drawing deeply on the smoke, he twisted around what he knew so far.

Dave Crone thought Marcus and Foley had killed Jefferson, and he was probably right. All else aside, Crone had fairly good instincts.

Someone was slaughtering horses on Bar C land and that just didn't seem fair to Slocum, killing a horse. It seemed to him that it was against God, somehow. Whoever was doing it, had to be doing it to hide what they were really up to.

And that brought him back to where he started and left him with as much as he had started with . . . which was little more than squat.

A horse racing up the road after him forced Slocum to turn in the saddle.

"Shit," he breathed.

Crone rode that poor short-legged bay of his at a hard gallop. Having few other options, Slocum reined Cougar to a stop. When Dave drew alongside of him, he demanded, "What the hell are you doin' here?"

"Figured you'd be headin' out to the ranch sometime today. Didn't figure it to be before the goddamn dawn, though, but I just slept in the livery, anyways, waitin' for you. What are you goin' to do when you get to the ranch?"

"I'm just goin' to have me a look-see. Go back to town." He gigged Cougar into a walk. "Ain't no need for you to ride with me right now."

"Maybe, maybe not. But I'm here, so the way I see it, ain't no need for me to go back to town."

Slocum was more than tempted to kick Cougar into a gallop, leaving Crone's horse scrambling to keep up, but that would draw a bit too much attention if anyone were watching the road. The dust cloud alone would be the visual equivalent of firing a cannon.

"Fine, Crone, but you keep your yap shut. I ain't in the mood to listen to you this mornin'."

Crone nodded. "Whatever you say, Slocum."

For once, Crone didn't babble, and after a few minutes, Slocum turned Cougar off the road and across country. Crone followed, still quiet.

Slocum turned in the saddle, leather creaking as he did. "Tell me again what you heard about Jefferson's killin'."

"Got hisself shot up by Marcus, over some dance-hall girl. Don't that beat all?"

"Did you see it?"

"Well, no," Crone admitted. "And I done told you that! But it come from a reliable source. Creed Norseman—you remember him. He saw the whole deal, and I never knew Creed to stretch a story in all his life. Heard tell, too, that Marcus was hooked with Foley, and that's right on the money."

Slocum didn't point out to Crone that Cassidy, the all around good soul and straight dealer whose range they were sneaking across, had seemingly hired Marcus and Foley.

Something still wasn't adding up right in Slocum's head.

Cougar snorted and shied back. Slocum reined in the Appaloosa, calming him. The breeze shifted, and the scent of blood and carrion carried with the wind.

They had to be close to the place where the horses were killed.

"Jesus, what's that smell?" Crone asked. His face screwed up. "It'd knock a buzzard off a goddamn shit wagon!"

"Shut up, Dave. That was the deal. You keep your pie hole closed and I let you tag along." Slocum put his heels lightly into Cougar's sides and the gelding unwillingly started forward again.

At the overlook of a deep ravine, the origin of the smell became apparent. Miranda's slaughtered horses littered the canyon floor. Slocum shook his head and felt anger twist at his stomach, felt his gorge rising. What a damned waste . . . and it still didn't make a blasted bit of sense.

He started Cougar down the slope of the ravine's wall, giving the animal his head. Crone followed, strangely and blessedly silent.

At the bottom of the ravine, Slocum swung down. Cougar snorted and danced, not wanting to go near the slaughtered animals. Slocum tied the gelding to a scrub pine and walked the remaining distance to the dead horses.

Crone didn't dismount. He kept peering up at the opposite rim of the ravine.

Buzzards and coyotes had just about finished what the butchers had started. Slocum turned on his heel. "Crone, if you were going to kill horses, why would you do it?"

Crone lifted his shoulders in a shrug and shook his head. "Ain't nobody got no need to be doin' that."

"Ain't nobody got a need to be doin' *this*," Slocum echoed. He walked back to Cougar, taking another long look around the ravine floor. "Somethin' tells me, this is a way to cover what's really happenin' here."

Slocum pulled Cougar's rein free, threw it across the horn, and then swung up. He turned the red dun from the carnage and started up the sloping ravine wall. Crone fell in behind.

Halfway up the slope, a shot rang out in the still-cool morning air. The red sandstone beside the Appaloosa exploded with a puff of dust. Slocum spurred Cougar and dropped low over the gelding's neck, urging him up the wall faster.

Crone's bay exploded past him, nimble as a mountain goat on the slippery sandstone. More shots peppered the ground.

As Crone's bay broke over the lip of the ravine wall, another shot caught Crone in the shoulder. He fell to one side, pulling the bay over. All Slocum could do was rein Cougar hard to the side and get out of the way of the falling horse.

Crone and his bay fell backward, tumbling over and over, ass over teakettle, all the way to the bottom of the ravine.

Cougar broke over the top of the wall, and Slocum spurred him to a protective outcropping. Vaulting from the saddle, he pulled his gun. He swept his hat off his head and peered around the rock to the opposite side of the ravine.

Nothing moved.

The Appaloosa breathed hard behind him, but didn't leave the protection of the rock outcrop. He was well trained to a ground tie.

Slocum was beyond angry. Whoever had taken shots at him and Crone knew he had been coming. Or at the very least, expected him to take a ride out to the Bar C.

When it became apparent that whoever had been on the opposite rim wasn't going to make the next move, Slocum debated his. He picked up his hat and cautiously extended it out enough to appear as if he was looking around the rock.

Nothing.

Well, whoever had been there was long gone by this time.

And they were taking their goddamn time about it, too. He couldn't even see the dust of their passing.

That, at least, would have given him something to follow.

He slammed his hat back on his head and stood up. He walked to the ravine rim. A look down at the floor told him there was nothing he could do for either Crone or Tommy, his bay.

Neither moved, and God surely never intended a man's head to be twisted so far around to the side as Crone's was.

"Dammit."

Slocum turned to Cougar and mounted. It had just become personal.

Passing the barkeep on his way to his room, Slocum demanded a bottle of whiskey. He marched up the stairs to his room.

Miranda was curled on the bed, naked as a jaybird, idly turning the pages of a book.

She looked up, her quirky smile crossing her face and just as quickly vanishing. "What happened, honey?"

Slocum didn't answer her. He pulled the cork from the neck of the bottle, spat it halfway across the room, and took a long pull. Lowering the bottle, he wiped his mouth with his shirtsleeve. "Who'd you tell you wired me?"

"No one. Except Carmelita, of course. And Berto, but he didn't believe me."

She sat up, flinging her hair off her shoulders. "Why? What happened?" she repeated.

"There's more to this than just horses gettin' killed. I took a ride out to the ranch, and got shot at. Dave Crone's dead."

"Dead?" She paled and pulled the sheet up around herself. "Someone shot him?"

Slocum nodded. "Winged him on a steep incline, which is about the same damned thing. He and his horse fell clear down the cliff. Did you know about Vance Jefferson gettin' killed?"

"I heard rumors." Miranda pulled her hair to a side, twisting it around her fingers, and her face fell. "Someone said he got called out over a dance-hall girl, but I can't believe that. He was like another uncle to me. And what's that have to do with us here?"

"Don't quite know, yet." Slocum took another long pull from the bottle. "Except your uncle hired the two boys what did it. At least, by all accounts. What could be on the Bar C worth killin' for?"

Miranda rose from the bed, wrapping the sheet around herself as she did. "Who?" she demanded. Slocum could practically see the wheels in her mind whirling. "Foley and Marcus?" she exclaimed at last. "Why, Vance was a good friend to Uncle Abel! And Vance Jefferson wasn't the kind to get himself killed over a saloon dancer. Besides, handcuffed and blindfolded, he could outdraw either Foley or Marcus!"

She sat back, huffing. "Now, I know he did some bad things when he was younger," she went on, "but ain't none of it somethin' that would make anybody want to murder him."

Miranda stood up and walked closer to Slocum, splaying her hand over his chest. "I was gettin' worried about you. And, I'm sorry about Crone. I guess you stopped at the sheriff's office on your way into town."

Slocum nodded. "Wasn't in. But the undertaker—and a deputy—are on the way out there now to get him. There's no way I could get him out of there with only my horse. Never would have made it back up the rise."

Miranda took the bottle from him and took a drink herself. "I'm just glad you're okay."

She handed the bottle to him and Slocum raised it to his lips. He paused. "Where were Marcus and Foley when Vance got killed?"

"They were over in New Mexico, on business. Uncle Abel sent them." She trailed off and her eyes narrowed. "Those *snakes*!"

"Not sure what I'm thinkin' just yet." He set the bottle on the small table near the window. "I'm thinkin' though, much as I hate to admit it, that you need to get some clothes on and we need to get out to your ranch."

Miranda sighed, flipped her hair off her shoulder, and flounced over to the bed. "And I'm thinkin' you're right. We're not goin' to find out anything here in town. Whatever it is that's worth killin' for is on the ranch. Maybe by way of going through Uncle Abel."

"Wish I knew what it is," Slocum admitted.

"You and me both. But if I find out that Marcus had anything to do with Vance's death, Uncle Abel will just kill him, himself."

Slocum laughed. "I don't doubt that for a second, honey."

5

"It'll just take me a minute to dress," Miranda said. While she pulled her saddlebags out from under the bed and laid them on the coverlet, Slocum took another long swig from his whiskey bottle.

Miranda opened the flaps and peered inside. From one of the pouches, she removed a checkered shirt and pair of britches. Quickly she drew on her shirt and worked the buttons closed.

Running her hands down her breasts and over her waist, she smoothed the wrinkles from the material.

Slocum glued his eyes to the long, muscular legs protruding from the bottom of that shirt. He swore, for such a little bit of a gal, Miranda was half legs. It wasn't the fashionable figure, but it did a whole heap for Slocum.

If not for the fact that they had to get moving, Miranda would have been in a heap of trouble.

Miranda bent over to pick up a pair of boots.

"Better hurry and cover up that pretty behind of yours, darlin'," he said, his voice tinged with regret.

Miranda responded with a deep-throated laugh and twisted her hips provocatively. Then she twirled, stuck out her lower lip, and raised her eyes to him. "You sure you can't spare one little minute, cowboy?"

Slocum gritted his teeth. Miranda could do things to a man in one of her minutes that took others a whole month of Sundays just to figure out.

Time for that later.

After a short search, Slocum retrieved the cork from underneath the bed, pressed it into the bottle, and set it on the night table. On second thought, he stuck the bottle inside one of his saddlebags.

In one fluid motion, Miranda stepped into the pants, yanked them over her hips, and buttoned them up. Then, twisting her hair into a loose knot, she secured it with her tortoiseshell pins.

"Ready?" she asked breathlessly.

"Yeah, ready." Slocum slung the saddlebags over his shoulder, grabbed his pack roll, and followed Miranda down the stairs.

"Looks a sight better than last night," Miranda said.

Someone had cleaned up the blood and straightened the tables and chairs. Saloon girls were notorious for sleeping late. They wouldn't stir for hours.

Miranda and Slocum crossed the barroom, but when they got to the doors, Slocum said, "Better let me go first. No sense in getting ourselves bushwhacked before we even leave town."

He swung open the doors and stepped onto the boardwalk. The street appeared normal, citizens going about their everyday business, except for the undertaker's wagon kicking up dust clouds just past the livery.

"I've been thinking," Miranda said. "Maybe we ought to take the other trail back to the Bar C."

"The one by the Indian ruins?"

Miranda flashed a smile. "You remember?"

"Sun ain't fried my brain yet." Yes, he remembered the ruins well. He'd be dead and halfway to hell—or Jesus—before he forgot the natural depression in the stream bed where he and Miranda had spent many lazy afternoons on his last visit to Apache Wells.

The trail was steeper and longer, but offered more cover if trouble found them.

At the livery, Toby, on Slocum's earlier orders, was just cinching the saddle on Miranda's gelding, one of the famous Cassidy quarter-milers. He was a tall palomino—called Sundancer, Toby had informed him—and a right good-looking piece of horseflesh, if Slocum was any judge. Which he was.

"Gotta knee him, Toby," Miranda said. "He's been sucking air when he feels the saddle."

Toby jabbed his knee into the horse's gut, and sure enough, they heard him snort out a stream of air. "Watered your horse, like you asked, Mr. Slocum. Sorry 'bout your friend."

Slocum nodded curtly and threw the saddlebags over Cougar's rump. Then he laced his fingers. "Leg up?" he asked.

Miranda placed her left knee in his hands. Then grabbing the reins and horn, she sprang upward, throwing her leg over the saddle. Slocum adjusted the stirrups, tossed a coin to Toby, and mounted Cougar.

"Looks like a hot one, Mr. Slocum."

Whether he meant the day or Miranda, Toby was dead on, Slocum thought.

He and Miranda followed the main road out of town for nearly a mile. But instead on the normal route to the Bar C, they turned onto a less used trail. Few of the locals even knew about it.

They'd still end up at the house, but from the north side of the ranch instead of the east.

"You haven't said much," Miranda remarked, sounding a touch worried.

"Just been thinkin'," he admitted. "Nothin' seems to add up yet. Now Dave Crone's dead, besides. Who'd want to shoot that old coot? He was annoying as a mosquito, but not enough so's you'd want to kill him." Slocum shook his head. "Hope your Uncle Abel don't mind—I told the undertaker to bring his body out to the Bar C for burial. You still got that cowboy's graveyard out there, don't you?"

Miranda reined in close and put a hand on his arm. "I'm sure he won't mind at all."

"Think it was the same person who killed Vance, Miranda?"

"That seems likely, but why?"

"What was Vance Jefferson doing in Apache Wells, anyhow?" Slocum opened his canteen, poured a little water on his bandanna, and wiped the back of his neck.

"Uncle Abel hired Vance about a year ago," she replied. "Vance claimed he was down on his luck. The way he looked, I doubted he'd had any kind of luck but bad for a long spell. But the last few weeks before Vance took off, they were quarrely as a couple of spinster sisters."

She shrugged her shoulders with a little shudder, as if it still bothered her a great deal.

In a moment, she continued, "Well, one morning, Uncle Abel had a mouse under his eye, and Vance was gone. I asked what happened, but he only grumbled something about letting the past stay buried. Most didn't know it, but those two went back a lot of years."

"Yeah," said Slocum.

"Sorry," Miranda said. "Forgot you knew them both from the olden times. But I remember my mother saying that Uncle Abel was a real pisser and sowed a lot of wild oats in his younger days. Even had a couple dimers written about him, before he settled down."

Slocum winced at the mention of the cursed novels, and wondered if Cassidy had grown to hate them half as much as he did. He also wondered if he should tell Miranda just how far back *he* went with them.

It wasn't exactly the time or place, he decided, and he asked, "What about the other two?"

"Marcus and Foley?" Miranda went on with a nod. "They're connected, too, somehow. They just showed up one day, demanding a job, and Uncle Abel gave it to them. Not a week after they started, the bunkhouse caught fire. Lucky that Vance came in right when it happened. Some fool left a pile of oily rags next to the stove. Vance put it out before there was any real damage. I heard him tell Uncle Abel that if those two didn't start it, they knew somethin' about it."

Slocum and Miranda crossed the stream that flowed down from the Indian ruins.

During the dry season, it was a mere trickle—or nothing at all—but there were times when a thunderstorm swelled it to a raging river, capable of sweeping away horses, wagons, and riders.

A flash of metal caught Slocum's eye. "Hold up a minute, Miranda. I see something." He slid from his saddle and bent to examine his find.

"What is it?"

"Well, I'll be a son of a bitch if somebody didn't drop a

twenty-dollar gold piece right here." Slocum walked behind Cougar and held the double eagle up to Miranda.
"Here. This belongs to you."

"Me? You're the one who found it."

"Yeah, but it was on Cassidy property."

"Don't be silly. No telling how long it's been there, who
it belonged to, or where it washed down from." She flipped
the coin into the air.

Slocum caught and pocketed the double eagle, then
picked up Cougar's reins and led him to the other side of
the wash. The sound of hooves scrambling on loose rocks
brought him to attention.

Miranda must have heard it, too. She sat frozen in her
saddle.

Slocum crouched beside the bank, put his finger to his
lips, and scanned the washout. Slowly he peered over the
edge. Then he laughed and stood, shaking his head. "Just a
few antelope."

Miranda's shoulders relaxed and she dug into her
horse's flanks with her heels. Clicking her tongue, she
urged him to climb the bank.

"Guess we're both a little jumpy, sweetie. I don't know
about you, but I'm ready to cool off," she called over her
shoulder.

By the time Slocum caught up, she had doffed her shirt
and loosed her hair. With that added bit of scenery, he def-
initely needed to cool off, too.

Tipping his hat back, he said, "Don't you know what
seein' you like this does to a man, Miranda? If you weren't
so damned pretty and so damned good at teasing, I'd have
half a mind to teach you a few manners."

She stared at him from flashing blue eyes. "And if you
try it, Mr. Slocum, you'll walk away with half a mind for

sure. Besides, if I was one of those hoity-toity girls, you'd be doin' your best to get me to be just like I am already. And for another thing, if you had *your* druthers, I know for a fact that you'd have me riding around naked as the day I was born, like that Lady Godiva woman, every chance you got."

After last night, how could she get him so randy? Miranda was right. A Miss Hoity-Toity would not suit him now. Not with Miranda Cassidy in his sights.

For longer than anyone could remember, the ruins had lain abandoned, their broken walls and crude windows slowly eroding in the wind and blowing sand.

Potsherds and piles of chert mixed with pieces of red rock littered the area. Discarded flint scrapers and the occasional quartz arrowhead poked out of the hardpan. Near an old fire pit, Slocum saw the half-carved bowl of a stone pipe.

Word had it the grounds were sacred, but it seemed the Anasazi held sacred everything they had ever touched. Or at least every blamed tribe that had come after them figured they did.

Miranda dismounted and pulled her saddlebags from her horse. She rummaged around until she found a rag and a bar of soap.

"I don't know about you, honey, but I'm not going another step till I have a bath—and not one of those horse trough affairs like you had yesterday."

Millennia of running water had gouged a hollow at the base of the rocks. Higher up, a small waterfall cascaded into it.

As Miranda talked, she slipped out of her pants and stepped into the pool. A gasp, like her pleasure noises from last night, escaped her lips.

"You coming, darlin'?" she purred and dipped under the water, rising again and grinning like she'd just found the sugar bowl full.

Slocum didn't need a second invitation. Quickly, he unbuckled his guns, stripped off his sweaty clothes, and joined Miranda in the pool. Sunlight sparkled like fresh-struck silver over the surface of the water.

Miranda ducked again and bobbed up a couple feet away from him. Holding up the rag and bar of soap, she taunted, "Ready for that bath, hombre?"

That was another thing he liked about Miranda. She was playful and creative, and right now she reminded him of Marta, the sloe-eyed beauty with nipples the size of dollars, from Santa Tourista. The so-called town was a watering hole for bandits and other unsavory trash, smack on the Mexican border, where the events of Slocum's visit had been immortalized in another dime saga—another series of brushes with death that fools mistook for adventure.

Slocum's hearty laughter echoed from the rocks. "*Sí, señorita*. This hombre's more than ready."

While he watched, Miranda first lathered her red tresses and then the washrag. Starting at the roots of her hair, she washed her face and neck and then tantalizingly cupped a breast.

She ran her tongue back and forth across her top lip as she circled the cloth round and round, first over one perfect orb, then the other.

Damn.

Her nipples stood up like two pink pebbles. Miranda stepped into the shallows and rested a slender foot on a rock. She soaped the rag again and washed her leg, then switched to the other.

Slocum stole up behind her and pinned her arms. Taking the washrag, he said, "Why don't you let me do that?"

She turned to face him, her body slippery from the water and suds. "Tell you what. I'll wash yours, if you wash mine . . . My back, of course. Fair, señor?"

Not at all fair. And holding on to her was about as likely as clinging to a greased pig at the county fair. If he'd thought he had a snowball's chance in hell, he would have taken her right where they stood.

She turned away and pulled her hair to the side. *"Gracias, gringo,"* she murmured as Slocum applied the cloth to her shoulders.

By the time he finished, she was thoroughly clean, and he was thoroughly hard and pressed tight against her backside. Slocum spun her around and lifted her, plastering a kiss on her mouth.

"¡Madre de Dios!" she said, breaking away. "Put me down, you beast!"

He momentarily tightened his arms around her, but then let her body slide down his chest. Miranda took him by the hand. Sashaying her hips seductively, she led him to a large, flat rock next to the stream. "I lied."

Slocum cocked his brow. "Lied?"

"You look surprised. But I know you'll be more than a mite glad." Miranda lay on her side and patted the rock. "And I will give you that bath . . . after I'm done with you."

Slocum stretched out beside her and drew her leg over his hips. "What in the Sam Hill has you so fired up?"

Her eyes half-lidded, Miranda nibbled his shoulder and pulled herself against him. She ground her heel into the small of his back. "I thought Slocum liked a bit of the salsa."

Her nails traced a scar on his side, souvenir from an Arkansas toothpick belonging to some egg-sucking dog in Wyoming a few years back.

He drove deep, the way she liked it—the way he liked it, too—and he pumped into her like a steam engine piston. She came fast and hard, and then came again before he found his release.

He lay on his back, the hot sun boring through his eyelids. A long, uninterrupted nap would be nice. He felt Miranda stand as he drifted off to sleep.

A sopping cold rag hit him square in the chest. "Wake up, Slocum. No time for daydreaming."

Miranda scrubbed the trail dust from every inch of his lean body. Lastly, she washed his balls and cock, and then the dark thatch of curls between his legs.

Slocum willed himself to stay calm. They had some riding to do before day's end.

As the sun sank behind the distant ridge of hills to the west, Miranda and Slocum crested a mound overlooking the house and outbuildings of the Bar C.

6

Uncle Abel must have seen them coming, for he was out in the yard to meet them when they rode in. His hat was pushed back, exposing his balding head, his skinny arms were spread wide, and a grin split his face.

"Slocum!" he cried. "So you're the surprise that Miranda's been tauntin' me with!"

Slocum slid off Cougar and walked forward, his smile almost as big as Abel Cassidy's. The men embraced briefly, than gleefully pounded each other's backs and shoulders until Miranda thought they'd kill each other. Or at least loosen a tooth or two.

She took Cougar's reins and led him and Sundancer over to the barn, where she handed them off to a stable hand, giving quiet instructions that Slocum's horse was to have the very best of care. She knew how Slocum was about his horses.

When she returned, Uncle Abel and Slocum were still standing and pounding and saying things like "By God!" and "Good to see you!" and "I'll be double-dogged!"

She shook her head.

Men.

Marching up to them, she grabbed hold of each of their back-slapping arms and said, "Why don't we go on up to the house before one of you fools knocks loose the other's lung?"

Both men laughed. It was good to see Uncle Abel in a happy mood for a change. It seemed he hadn't smiled in a coon's age. And she always liked to see Slocum happy. Grinning, she led on.

She landed them on the wide porch and called to Carmelita for a pitcher of lemonade, a flask of bourbon, and three glasses. They'd need something a little stronger than plain lemonade to hash this thing out.

And then she sat down with them, propped her elbows on the table, and listened.

"Can't talk you out of those damned spotted horses, can I, Slocum?" Abel was saying, shaking his head.

Slocum grinned. "Not till you find me one as mountain-goat nimble on a rocky slope or as puss-cat easy-goin', Abel."

He'd had this conversation with Abel more times than he could count. Every meeting between the two of them started with it, and every parting ended on the same note. Truth was, Slocum wouldn't have taken another breed of horse if it was given to him, tied up in a bow, and strung with twenty-dollar gold pieces.

But he never said as much, not to Abel.

He had known Abel for—what was it now?—must be over twenty years. They'd met up when Slocum first came west, back in the sixties, after the war, when Abel was part of the Jorge Mondragon gang. Slocum had joined up, and they'd done some damage to the Territory, all right. They called themselves Mondragon's Dragons. Thought it was kind of funny at the time.

They met Vance Jefferson then, too. Vance was a slick hand with a gun—nearly as good as Slocum himself, which was saying quite a bit.

Later, after Mondragon got himself hanged down in Sonora, the three men had ridden together for a while. But pretty soon Jefferson dropped off to head for California, and Cassidy settled down to raise horses with his brother, Miranda's father.

Slocum had gone his own way.

And had been going that way ever since.

They met up again, two at a time, on rare occasions: mostly Slocum and Jefferson, for whom California hadn't turned out to be the Golden State after all. And on one of those meetings, they'd run into Bob Marcus and Granger Foley. Well, Marcus, really. They always seemed to miss Foley by just minutes.

After all, the Arizona Territory was a sparsely populated chunk of land, even nowadays. Back then, it had been practically desolate. It figured that everybody, especially traveling men, would know just about everybody else in the whole territory.

Slocum had taken a distinct dislike to Foley right off the bat—mostly because he never showed up—and he wasn't awful crazy about Marcus, either. The two men were thick as thieves even back then, and showed little enthusiasm for stopping the range war they had been hired to stop.

They showed a great deal more excitement come payday.

Foley was a hired gun who held up stages in his spare time, and he wasn't shy talking about it. Marcus was more closemouthed, but Slocum figured his background to be about the same as Foley's. He was too fast with a gun to be an amateur.

Now, by this time, there had been enough water under the proverbial bridge that Slocum wasn't the same man he'd been when he first came west. He wasn't bitter anymore—not about the war, not about his papa's and brother's murders or the theft of the family farm.

Well, all right, he was still bitter about his father and brother.

But it wasn't anything he couldn't live with. He'd stopped robbing and killing—except when he was certain he was on the side of right, as in that range war he was trying to break up back then—and was doing his best to live straight.

And so he might have been a little harder on Marcus and Foley than usual.

Still, the pair of them had left a bad taste in his mouth. Just the mention of their names still did.

Abel had about finished the Great Quarter-mile Running Horse vs. Appaloosa debate all on his own, and Slocum decided it was time to broach the subject of the business at hand.

"Abel," he said, "you remember Vance Jefferson?"

Cassidy's face screwed up momentarily, and then he said, "Well, sure! Ol' Mondragon's gang!"

"He's dead, Uncle Abel," said Miranda, and refilled her glass with lemonade.

"Well, of course he is! Got hanged in New Mexico, didn't he, Slocum?" Cassidy exclaimed, and glared at Miranda as if she were an idiot.

"No, no, Abel," Slocum said. "Vance Jefferson's dead. Dave Crone told me that Bob Marcus and Granger Foley were responsible."

"Dead, you say?" Cassidy railed. "What on earth? Why, he worked on this place for a while, worked right here! And who the hell is Dave Crone?"

Slocum's brow furrowed. "He's the man I rode up here with. The man that was murdered on your land just this mornin'."

Cassidy drew himself up, and Slocum quickly explained the whole deal. When he was done, Cassidy was slumped in his chair and shaking his head. "Damn," he kept repeating. "Damn! The undertaker was here with a body, but I just thought he was some saddle tramp that got himself killed fallin' down a cliff! Now, if he'd been ridin' one of my quarter-mile horses . . ."

"You've got to fire Marcus and Foley, Uncle Abel," said Miranda. "Now."

He looked up. "Can't do that, girl."

"But why?"

"Because of these blasted horse killers!" he snapped. "At least I can trust Marcus and Foley to patrol for them. It takes a killer to catch a killer, y'know, and I heard of Marcus and Foley before they ever rode in here!" he added, belatedly.

"Point taken, Abel," interjected Slocum. "But still, I'd keep a real close eye on those boys. I figure they shot Crone. Don't know who else'd do it."

Except maybe me, he thought, *just to shut him up . . .*

And then he said, "Listen, Abel. I'll take care of these horse killers for you. You don't need Marcus and Foley."

"Be pleased if you'd help, Slocum," Abel said, "but she's more'n a one-man job. Hell, they're cuttin' 'em up into steak and leavin' 'em all over the ranch." Suddenly, he threw both hands into the air. "Some people are just plain lunatic crazy!"

Miranda leapt to her feet, and Slocum quickly poured Abel's glass half-full of bourbon. Arms around his neck, Miranda calmed her agitated uncle down, and Slocum offered his drink.

"Sorry," Abel said after a moment had passed and the bourbon had had a chance to take hold. "It just makes me so goddamned mad!"

"I know, dear," Miranda said soothingly, stroking his arm. "Makes you feel helpless, too, doesn't it?"

Abel sniffed.

Slocum said, "Well, that's about to end, ol' buddy. And I'm stickin' around until it does."

Miranda settled Slocum into the guest room, a dark blue–papered affair set all around with dark, heavily carved, ornate furniture.

"Why here?" he asked. They had passed a number of empty rooms on their way down the hall. "I feel like I'm a guest at the undertaker's place."

"Because it's the farthest from Uncle Abel's," she said, and smiled at him. And then winked. "When you're settled, come on out. Carmelita ought to have lunch on the table pretty soon."

Then she slipped out the door.

More's the pity.

It didn't take Slocum long to unpack. He simply slung his saddlebags on the bed and shoved his pack roll into the chifforobe.

He removed his hat, quickly ran a comb through his dark and unruly hair, wiped his dusty boots on the skirt of the bedspread—also dark blue—and then pulled the double eagle from his pocket.

Right odd, that anybody would lose one of these and not

miss it. It was almost the size of a silver cartwheel and weighty to boot, and a man would know it was gone.

And furthermore, what call would a man have to take it out of his pocket in the middle of nowhere?

Shaking his head, he stuck the coin back where he'd found it and left the room.

Carmelita was, indeed, setting the table when he came out. The smell of enchiladas, which he had noticed on his way through the house before, now filled the air as she set the platter on the table.

He smiled. Judah Cassidy, Miranda's daddy, had snared himself a good cook, and he—and then his brother—had managed to keep her for almost twenty years. Plates of corn tortillas and flour sat round the table, as did a large bowl of refritos and another of rice. Smaller bowls of guacamole and salsa and cactus jelly filled in the cracks.

Despite himself, Slocum licked his lips.

Cassidy's voice came from behind him. "She's awful good, our Carmelita."

"I remember," Slocum said, and grinned.

Miranda poked her head in from the kitchen, looked at the floor, then up at Slocum. "Spurs?"

He'd forgotten.

He sat down in the nearest chair, which just happened to be at the dining room table, and removed them. "When you usually dine on the prairie," he began, by way of apology, "you sort of lose track—"

"Of the finer things." Miranda cut in, grinning. "Like civilization and polished wood floors. I know. You're forgiven. At least you didn't wear your hat."

She didn't know how close he'd come to it, but he just smiled at her.

The meal was so good that Slocum didn't take the time

to talk. He just shoveled in that good Mexican cooking and occasionally asked for more lemonade, please. He'd noticed that Abel had planted a whole grove of lemon and lime trees out west of the house and that they were all heavy with spring fruit, so he wasn't afraid of depleting the supply.

When they were almost finished with the meal and Slocum was happily digging into his flan—which was served with extra caramel sauce—there came a knock at the front door. Miranda excused herself and answered it, and when Slocum saw who it was, he stopped eating.

Bob Marcus.

He stepped into the house, with Foley right behind him.

Slocum stood up.

They stared at Slocum first with surprise and then with bad intentions—and he stared back with worse—until Abel cheerily said, "I believe you fellers know each other!"

Slocum let himself take a breath when Marcus and Foley relaxed. His hand never strayed far from his Colt, though.

"Yeah," Marcus said, with little enthusiasm, then turned toward Abel. "We got one'a your horse butcherers this morning."

"You don't say!" Abel said. "Where? Did you catch him in the act?"

"Not exactly. But he was on your land, and near the canyon," Marcus said.

"We got his horse, too," added Foley smugly. "Served the horse-killin' bastard right!"

"Just thought you'd like to know, Mr. Cassidy," added Marcus, who then shot a daggered glance at Slocum.

"That was no horse killer, you idiots," Slocum said, trying his best to keep his tone even, although the thing he wanted most in the world was to take these two outside and pummel them to death with an ax handle.

"Huh?" said Foley, with his usual keen wit and quick intelligence.

"You killed Dave Crone, you lunatics!" said Slocum. "Dave Crone. You remember Dave Crone, don't you, Marcus?"

Marcus had the good sense to appear puzzled. "Sure, but . . . why would Dave Crone be killin' our horses?"

Slocum was too angry to speak, but Abel quickly said, "I think you made a mistake, boys. Crone was on his way out to the ranch—with Slocum, here—to pay me a visit."

Miranda nodded sagely.

Foley stared at his feet.

Marcus growled, "Right sorry about that, Mr. Cassidy. He was pretty far off from us. But you can't expect that we'd spy a man that close to the canyon and not think he was one'a the ones we've been lookin' for!"

"I suppose not," Abel admitted. Slocum noticed, however, that at least Abel didn't invite them to stay for a meal.

Miranda ushered both men back outside, then returned to the table and shook out her napkin.

"The plot thickens," she said softly, smoothing her napkin in her lap.

"Yes, it does," growled Slocum, who was still grinding his teeth.

"More flan, anybody?" asked Abel, helping himself.

"That all it means to you, Abel?" Slocum asked, more sternly than he'd intended. "Two men confess in your parlor to a cold-blooded murder, and all you can think about is more flan? Hell! I'm surprised you didn't ask 'em in to take lunch with us!"

Waving a spoonful of the caramel custard before his face, Abel said, "Couldn't see that it'd do anybody any good to start a gunfight in the house, Slocum. Things'll get cleared up in time."

He slid the spoon and its contents into his mouth, chewed exactly twice, then swallowed. "All in good time."

Miranda nodded, although somewhat dubiously. "Whatever you say, Uncle Abel."

7

Slocum discovered that he'd suddenly lost his appetite. He stood, grabbing his spurs from the corner of the table, and left the dining room. He went out onto the porch and rolled a smoke.

He pulled a long, calming drag, forcing himself to keep a lid on his temper. Leaning one arm onto the porch railing, he contemplatively smoked the quirlie.

A loose board creaked with Miranda's tread, and her small hand brushed across the width of his shoulders. "Honey, he's tryin' to do what's right."

"If he was, he'd be firin' those two and movin' 'em on down the road. We both know that. And if this is how he acts when one of his oldest friends gets shot, I sure don't need him coverin' my back."

"Now, Slocum . . ."

He shoved off the porch railing. "Don't."

Miranda had the good sense not to press him, for which he was thankful. He picked up his spurs and buckled them on.

"I'm goin' to take another ride around and see what I can shake loose. Cougar's in a stall?"

Miranda nodded, but didn't follow him off the porch. "Just be careful, John."

He paused. The fact she'd used his given name was enough to bring him up short. She had to be really worried if she did that.

He managed a smile.

"Hey, honey, I'm always careful. That's why I'm still alive."

Slocum made his way to the barn. Cougar was in a roomy box stall, contentedly munching his way through a bucket of ground corn and oats. "You got the five-star treatment, didn't you, buddy?"

Cougar didn't bother to lift his nose from the feed bucket. Slocum walked down the long, wide aisle of the barn to the tack room. His saddle and blanket had been placed on a rack, the bridle draped over the seat. He picked up the saddle, the blanket, and a bristle brush and went back to Cougar.

The Appaloosa still didn't greet him. He was too busy licking the last grains of feed from the bottom of the bucket. Slocum started brushing the gelding, pulling the dust of the trail from the horse's neck.

As he swept the brush in long strokes over the gelding, dust rose and flew from Cougar's broad back. Slocum brushed until a sheen glistened over the snowflake patterning on the gelding's rump.

He set the brush on the stall wall, placed the blanket on Cougar's back, and smoothed it out. When he was satisfied it was flat, he lowered the saddle over the blanket.

Cougar rolled his eyes and drew a deep breath.

"Yeah, suck up the air . . ." Slocum pulled the cinch

tight, and while he waited, he picked out the gelding's hooves. After a while, Cougar had to release the breath he held, and Slocum took up the remaining slack in his girth.

"No need to ever knee a horse, is there, buddy? Just gotta wait till nature takes its course."

He slipped the bridle up Cougar's head, and the gelding took the bit. He led the horse from the stall and down the wide aisle.

Outside the barn in the noonday sun, Slocum paused before swinging up. He lifted Cougar's right front leg, bending it at the knee and raising it as high as it would go. He ran his hand along the girth, assuring himself the wide leather wasn't pinching Cougar anywhere.

He'd forgone this one procedure once and had a horse with a massive cinch burn that had laid the animal up for nearly a week while it healed. Ever since, he'd made sure the cinch didn't pinch.

As he swung up, he realized he was missing his hat. He dropped back to the ground and threw Cougar's left rein around the hitching rail. Muttering to himself, he made his way to the house, down the hall to the room Miranda had put him in, and grabbed his hat off the corner post of the bed.

Settling it onto his dark hair, he left the house, ignoring Abel's calls of "Slocum, hey . . . Slocum!"

Abel was not the person he wanted to talk to at the moment. If the man had even a lick of sense, he'd figure that out and let him cool off.

Finally swinging up on Cougar, he turned the Appaloosa's head to the east and kneed him into a slow, easy lope. As soon as the gelding settled into the rocking motion, Slocum felt some of the tension lifting from the back of his neck.

Someone had once said that the outside of a horse was

good for the inside of a man, and Slocum was not one to argue with that wisdom.

The Bar C was a huge spread. He knew he couldn't ride even a quarter of the fence-line in one day, but he had no intention of riding the perimeter of the ranch. He knew there was another way into that ravine where some of the dead horses were, and he wanted to have another gander at the place.

He doubted he'd find anything that would shed more light onto this puzzle, but he wanted to rule out a few things, too.

Before he had ridden halfway to the ravine, sweat was dripping down Slocum's back and trailing down his face from his temples and nose. Not bothering to rein Cougar in, he pulled his hat off, wiped his brow and face with his shirtsleeve, and readjusted his hat.

Cougar was sweating, but he wasn't breathing hard, and the gelding wasn't lathered, either. This pace was easy enough on him.

At the back entrance to the ravine, Cougar slowed his own gait. His head came up and he snorted, shying back several steps and turning in a tight circle.

If anything, the stench of carrion was stronger than it had been that morning.

Slocum patted the gelding's shoulder. "I know, buddy. Just stay calm, because I'm goin' to ask you to go back there."

As if he understood every word, the gelding tossed his head in objection and spun again.

"Hey, you know what, you'd make a right fine cuttin' horse if you could do that with cattle," Slocum assured the horse, guiding him through the spin and down into the ravine.

Cougar's ears flicked rapidly from front to back, as if he, too, was alert to any threat. He danced across the chert and sandstone floor, his head bobbing and ears flicking, his shoes clattering. At the far end of the ravine, Dave Crone's gelding, stripped of its tack, lay with its legs straight out from its body.

Slocum ground his teeth.

"Those damn idiots."

Cougar tossed his head as if he agreed.

When they emerged from the ravine, Slocum pulled Cougar to a stop. He scanned the ravine walls, but could see nothing out of the ordinary. Whatever the horses were killed for wasn't in this canyon.

There were a few of those bizarre Indian etchings on the walls, but nothing that Slocum hadn't seen a few hundred times in nameless canyons dotting the Arizona landscape. He'd often wondered if the etchings in the rocks had been the Indians' way of putting up "wanted" posters, or a way to announce some major community event to everyone.

That thought made him grin a little. "Yeah. Forget smoke signals . . . just check out the town paper . . . carved weekly on a canyon wall. 'Heap big hunt next week. Raid white settlement tomorrow night.'"

Cougar snorted.

"You don't think that's funny?" Slocum started Cougar forward again. "Well, I don't know a lot of horses who have a sense of humor, so you ain't got room to talk, buddy."

He cut across the ranch, going back to the way he and Miranda had ridden in that morning. The sun beat down from the sky, pulsing white and blistering hot. Not even a lizard stirred in the heat of the afternoon.

Slocum debated the smarts of being out in the desert in

the heat of the day, but figured as long as Cougar wasn't getting too hot, he could tough it out.

He passed a large stand of saguaro. A woodpecker of some sort perched on the top of one, then wobbled its way down to a hole drilled into the cactus and vanished inside.

High overhead, a hawk drifted lazily across the endless expanse. A moment later, the predator folded its wings and dropped like a bullet to the ground.

Slocum watched as the big bay-wing rose a few moments later with empty talons. He grinned. Even the best of them sometimes missed.

He couldn't recall a time when a riverbed lined with cottonwoods had looked so inviting . . . other than that morning, he qualified. Cougar waded into the middle of the small stream. Slocum dropped the reins and let the horse drink.

He looked around, noting the high walls, with stone carved into graceful curves and deep bowls by ages of running water. Cottonwoods lined the streambed and crept partially up the sides of the canyon. Their leaves filtered the blazing sun into a cool light, the color of buttered limes.

It was better than sitting in church, Slocum decided, and probably a whole lot closer to the Almighty.

And that brought him back to Dave Crone, who probably hadn't had much of a service said over him. And a bunch of dead, butchered horses. And one hefty, shiny twenty-dollar gold piece.

And Vance Jefferson.

And, somehow . . . though he was damned if he knew how yet, they were all intertwined.

Slocum swung off Cougar and walked slowly along the bank of the tiny, trickling creek, leading the Appaloosa. He hadn't walked far when another glint of gold in the bottom of the streambed caught his eye.

"What in the hell . . ."

He bent and picked up another twenty-dollar gold piece. He shot a glance up and down the creek. There was no way on God's green earth a wagon could have maneuvered its way along this riverbed. It was too narrow for one thing, and for another, it was way too uneven.

The wagon would have broken its wheels, at the least . . . an axle was more like it.

He flipped the coin into the air. The green-filtered sunlight caught on its edges, which glinted brightly. Slocum caught the coin in his palm, kneeling as he did.

Now, one large twenty-dollar gold piece *might* have fallen from someone's pocket . . . but two? Highly unlikely. Slocum slowly scanned the creek bed, then the canyon walls. Dead horses, dead men, hired guns, gold pieces . . .

The dead horses were a diversion, plain and simple. Slocum was sure of that now. But a diversion from what? He rocked back onto his heels. Foley robbed stages and Marcus was probably involved with more than one stage robbery with Foley. Among other things.

Where did Vance Jefferson fit into it, though? And, if the horses were a diversion, why had those jackasses killed Dave Crone and tried to kill Slocum, too? There was no way he and Crone could have learned anything over in the ravine where the dead horses were.

Slocum ran his thumb along the rim of the gold piece. Crone had seemed mighty jumpy that morning, down in the ravine. Kept looking around him, as if he was expecting someone to start shooting.

Slocum stood and swung up onto Cougar. He gently

urged him into a slow walk, letting the horse pick his way across the slippery wet chert and sandstone.

Slocum used the time to really study the canyon walls. And the whole way to the path where he and Miranda had entered the canyon, there was nothing he could say stood out in any way.

Rather than turn out onto the narrow path, he continued along the canyon floor.

Here, the cottonwoods grew thicker and the stream was a little deeper. The trees were also larger, older, and had grown more gargoylish in their effort to reach the sunlight.

A few feet on and the trees seemed to have grown first to the ground and then to the sunlight. They were actually twisted completely around, gnarled and bent in their effort to grow upward.

Cougar halted, swaying his head from side to side. Slocum sucked a long breath in, fighting nausea. Without any command, the Appaloosa backed up the stream and the nausea vanished.

"Bad medicine in there," Slocum muttered. "What the hell is that place?"

Slocum gigged Cougar forward and the horse completely balked.

Slocum huffed out a little sigh. "All right, old son. I can take the hint. We ain't goin' back in there."

He turned the horse around and went back the way they had come. He had passed the small path again when Cougar pulled up short.

The horse stood as if frozen, his ears perked straight ahead. He raised his head and took a deep breath, then snorted and backed a step.

Slocum also noted that not a bird chirped. When he had

passed through a short while ago, birds had been jabbering to one another all through the shaded, cool canyon.

This silence was unnerving. He slid a hand down to his gun and slipped it from the holster.

"Come on, ol' son, let's go."

Cougar still balked, but now his ears were swiveling from side to side. Slocum looked slowly from one side to the other. He couldn't see a damn thing other than cottonwoods.

He lightly pressed the blunted rowels of his spurs into Cougar's sides. "Git up, Cougar."

The Appaloosa took one step forward, and then backed several steps as fast as he could.

"Dammit, you're goin' to make me lead you, ain't you?"

Slocum swung down and started walking. Actually, he felt a little more confident. While he didn't want anything to happen to Cougar, at least the horse's size alone offered him some protection if anyone was up on those walls looking to be shooting down into the canyon.

He had reached the pool where he and Miranda had spent a very pleasant few hours, when Cougar came to a dead halt again. This time, the Appaloosa rose up off his front legs. Slocum was pulled off his feet, but he hung onto the reins.

And now Slocum could smell what Cougar had smelled. The warm, metallic scent of fresh blood assaulted him. No wonder the horse wouldn't go forward.

And he wasn't about to leave Cougar to go investigate. He probably didn't have to go see what had spilled that much blood. He could make a pretty good guess.

Slocum led Cougar back to the path. Well, hell, he could take the long way back to the ranch house. Just meant he'd probably miss supper. Provided he got out of the canyon alive.

Every hair on the back of his neck was standing up, tingling with warning. He was being forced to the path. He couldn't go either way along the canyon floor.

Before he left the protection of the trees, Slocum swung up onto Cougar. He patted the gelding's neck. "Ol' buddy, you are goin' to have to run your damn legs off in a minute or two. You ready for this?"

Cougar danced under him. He had never seen the horse this spooky. Cougar usually was as calm as a spinster's parlor on a Sunday afternoon.

Slocum pointed him at the trail and kicked the gelding into an all-out gallop. Cougar exploded under him, more than ready to leave the canyon. As they broke the tree line, one shot rang out.

Slocum felt the bullet burn across his upper arm. He crouched down lower on Cougar's neck, lashing him with the reins. He risked a glance back, looking under his arm, not wanting to expose his head.

Whoever had taken that shot was well hidden in the trees. And also didn't have a clean shot, because of those trees. He knew only one . . . no, make that two men who were so adept at ambushing people from the protection of a copse of trees.

He spared a look at his upper arm. Blood ran down his sleeve. It didn't seem to be much more than a flesh wound, but the shirt was ruined. Dammit, he'd just bought the thing down in Monkey Springs! Paid extra for its "durability," too.

So much for that!

He reined Cougar to a stop, spinning him around to the copse of cottonwoods. Nothing moved, not even a leaf on a single tree.

This was getting too goddamn old.

He was tired of getting shot at and not being able to return the favor.

Slocum turned Cougar and gigged him into an easy lope. This time, when he got to the ranch, there was going to be hell to pay.

8

On another part of the ranch, Bob Marcus and Granger Foley were doing a little sightseeing of their own. Foley had been at it for hours. Marcus had just galloped up a few minutes ago, and his horse was lathered and blowing.

He paid the gelding little mind, though.

He busied himself doing much the same as Foley: They rode slowly, eyes tightly focused on the landscape, hopping down every once in a while to investigate a rock that seemed out of place or a cubbyhole in the sandstone outcrop.

After about an hour of this, it was starting to get dark, and Foley had finally had it. "Where the hell'd he put it?" he yelled.

"Quiet, you fool!" snapped Marcus.

"Aw, who's gonna hear me way the hell out here?"

"You never can tell."

Foley twisted up his face and wobbled it from side to side, mocking Marcus. "You never can tell, you never can tell," he parroted before he grew serious again. "I still say it's in the house somewhere. We should turn that place upside down!"

"Jefferson already did," Marcus replied.

"How do you know that?"

"He told me so. And before you say anything else, Jefferson was a lot of things, but he wasn't a liar. And he had as much of a stake in this deal as we do."

"You're a fool, Marcus," Foley said with a snort, and got back up on his horse. He glanced up at the sky. "Time for us to quit playin' hide-and-seek. Gonna be full dark by the time we get back."

"Yup," Marcus said, and reined his tired horse around. "Race you?"

"Not on your life. That nag of yours'd drop dead before we got a hundred yards. You're hell on a horse, Marcus."

"Guilty as charged," Marcus said, and pushed his mount into a jog.

Shaking his head, Foley followed along.

"Miranda!"

At the sound of her uncle's call, Miranda stood up from her dressing table, where she had been brushing her long, unruly curls, and went to the door. She stuck her head out and yelled, "What, Uncle Abel?"

"Come out for a second. I want to talk to you."

"All right," she said, pushing her hair over her shoulders.

With Uncle Abel, you could never be certain whether he wanted to upbraid you for something stupid, or whether he just wanted to pass the time of day. In either case, he didn't like to be put off by something so silly as a girl wanting to fix her hair up.

When she reached the parlor, she found him standing in the center of the room, arms firmly crossed, tapping his foot. It looked like he was primed to holler, but she couldn't be sure why.

Maybe he'd found out that she was sleeping with Slocum. But how? Who could have told him? They hadn't done a thing here at the ranch—yet—and he hadn't been to town in a coon's age.

She took a deep breath and said, "Yes, Uncle Abel? What is it?"

He turned toward her, and his face was deadly serious. A part of her relaxed. It wasn't about Slocum, anyway. If it were, he would have been furious, not serious.

With Abel Cassidy, there was a very large difference.

"Miranda," he began, "why is Slocum here?"

She stood her ground. "Because I wired him to come. I was upset about the horses, and I didn't think your men were moving fast enough."

His brow furrowed. "And just what business is that of yours, anyhow? Seems to me this is my ranch, not the Miranda Cassidy Spread."

"I thought it was going to be mine someday, Uncle Abel," she said firmly. "I just wanted there to be something for you to leave me, that's all."

"Well, I want him out of here."

"Slocum? Why on earth?"

Cassidy paused a moment, as if thinking. Then he said, "He's trouble, that's why."

"Oh, pish!"

"Don't you 'oh, pish' me, young lady! I want him gone by morning, you hear me?"

Miranda ground her teeth and felt her hands tighten into fists. Uncle Abel could make her upset, but he'd never made her so downright mad before!

"Uncle Abel, this place is as much mine as yours. My

daddy owned half of it before he got killed. And I want Slocum to stick around. Frankly, I think your Marcus and Foley are a couple of scoundrels. For all I know, they're killing our horses themselves!"

He took a step toward her. "You watch your mouth, girl!"

"I will not! And I won't tell Slocum to go, and you won't either."

With that, she turned away from him and marched back to her room, ignoring his shouts of "Miranda! Miranda! Get back out here!"

Damn, but he could be pigheaded!

Slocum jogged into the ranch's yard just as the sun was casting the last rays of wildly colored light over the western horizon. He put up Cougar, giving him a good rubdown and a ration of oats, then headed to the house.

He smelled dinner before he opened the door. Fried chicken was his guess, and when he opened the door and got a gander at the table, he learned he was right.

Abel was just sitting down, and Miranda, her hair piled on top of her head in ringlets and wearing a pretty blue dress, was coming up the hall.

She smiled at him.

"Howdy, Slocum," she said. "How did it go?"

Belatedly, he swept off his hat. "Howdy, Miranda, Abel." Abel had yet to acknowledge him, but then, there was that chicken . . .

He said, "Not much. Got shot at again, though."

Miranda's face was suddenly filled with alarm. "Are you all right?"

He twisted his arm to show where his shirt was torn and

bloody. "Just hit the fat. Whoever it was, he was hidin' in the cottonwoods. Couldn't make 'im out, let alone spot 'im to shoot back."

Miranda led him to a chair and saw to his arm. As far as he was concerned, it could have waited. That fried chicken was fairly driving him crazy. Abel, who was totally ignoring both him and Miranda, was going to eat the entire hen before he got a chance at it!

At last, Miranda tied off the wound and said, "Eat, Slocum!"

He dived in directly. Three pieces of chicken, a mound of mashed potatoes, a few ladles of gravy, and half the remaining peas—that was just for starters. He'd worked up an appetite.

He caught Miranda out of the corner of his eye, just looking at him and grinning. He shot her back a slightly embarrassed smile, but he kept on shoveling in the food. And thankfully, Carmelita wandered in a few minutes later with new bowls and platters of everything.

He paused about halfway through the proceedings to ask, "Anything new from your boys, Abel?"

But Abel looked up at him from beneath beetling brows and just grunted. Odd.

He flicked a look at Miranda, who silently mouthed, "Later."

By the time they'd finished dinner and the table was cleared, Abel still hadn't spoken to him. Neither had he offered brandy or cigars. So Slocum made a show of stretching his arms and remarking on how tired he was, then ambled down the hall.

He went to his room and sat on the bed, waiting for Miranda. She turned up a minute later with two brandies, one for each of them, and one of Abel's specially blended cigars for Slocum.

He took both gratefully. The cigars weren't the best, but they were a welcome change from the quirlies he usually smoked, especially when enjoyed with a good glass of brandy.

"What the hell's the matter with your uncle Abel tonight?" he grumbled, after he'd bit the end off his cigar and lit it.

Miranda had yet to settle anywhere and was pacing the room. Shaking her head, she said, "I don't know. I can't figure it out. I mean, why he'd be so . . ."

"So what?"

"So . . . adamant! So cranky! And so . . . mean!" She took a deep breath. "Slocum, he wants you out of here in the worst way."

Slocum arched a brow. "But he wants Marcus and Foley to stay?"

Artlessly, Miranda dropped down into a chair. "Yes. If you can believe that!"

"I'm tryin' to."

Actually, it didn't make any sense at all. Not unless Abel was up to something with Marcus. Or Foley. Or both.

But what? He couldn't picture Abel Cassidy doing any sort of business with those two. But then, he'd hired them on, hadn't he?

Now, Vance Jefferson had been a good friend to Abel Cassidy. They went back a long, long way. But Abel had taken the news that Jefferson had been murdered by Marcus and Foley in much the same way he'd take the news that the sun was shining today.

Slocum shook his head. "Miranda, honey, there's somethin' goin' on here, but I'll be damned if I can figure out what!"

He said nothing more, but he had decided he needed to take a new look at his old friend Abel.

Marcus and Foley rode into the ranch about a half hour after Slocum and put their horses away. Foley made an attempt to brush his horse, but Marcus just tied his gelding and walked off.

"You're hell on a horse, Marcus," Foley muttered once more, under his breath, and brushed down Marcus's horse after he'd finished with his own.

He found Marcus in the bunkhouse, already deep in his cups.

Somebody had hauled out a jug of white lightning, and the boys were taking full advantage of it. It was the first and only liquor they'd seen on the ranch since they started working there. Usually, he and Marcus had to ride into town to get a belt.

Well, let Marcus have his drink. Foley was more interested in dinner.

He went to the cookstove, grabbed himself an enameled plate, filled it with beans, salt pork, and bread, poured himself a cup of coffee, and went to his bunk to eat in peace. The men were getting rowdy now, telling tall tales and acting some of them out.

He hoped to hell that Marcus didn't get to talking. Marcus might be a fool about some things, but he should know when to keep his mouth shut.

Shouldn't he?

Foley had been a callow youth of twenty-three when he, Marcus, Abel Cassidy, Vance Jefferson, and Bill Buckley had held up the *Butterfield* out of Flagstaff and made off with the Double Aces payroll. It was quite a bit of money, and there was no time to split it up. Buckley's horse was the only one strong enough to carry his rider and the payroll for any distance, too.

They had all ridden in different directions, but unbeknownst to any of them, Buckley had made straight for the Cassidy spread. Abel and his brother had the property, even back then. And Buckley had buried the payroll somewhere on that land.

It was a smart move, except that Buckley hadn't counted on being drawn on and killed by an upstart gunslinger the very next week—right after he'd run into Jefferson and told him what he'd done.

The bad news was that he hadn't told Jefferson exactly *where* he'd hidden the money.

Foley figured that payroll had to be about $50,000. The Double Aces mine had been an awful big operation in its day. Fifty thousand, just sitting out there someplace, probably with a rattler nesting right on top of it—

Damn!

The horse killing—now, that had been Marcus's idea. Foley didn't hold with it just on general principle, but by the time he heard about it, it was too late.

He supposed that to Marcus, anything that moved was fair game.

Marcus called it a "diversion." And he sure took advantage of it, saying, "Well, hell, ol' Abel didn't have the sense to raise cattle. You wouldn't've minded me shooting a little beef, now, would you?"

Foley had to agree.

After all, you didn't quarrel with Marcus, not if you knew what was good for you.

What really bothered him, though, was that Marcus went down after he'd made the kill and well . . . had his way with the dead animals. Then he practically chopped steaks out of the carcasses and carried the meat out into the brush, where he left it for the coyotes.

To Foley, it was sacrilege. Every single nasty part of it.

But at least the coyotes were happy.

Foley figured that Marcus was going to stop killing horses now that Slocum was around.

At least, he hoped so. Marcus didn't talk much, but it seemed like he knew Slocum pretty damn well. Foley had only just heard about him a long time back, and he'd always wished they'd meet so he could ask for his autograph.

Just for a conversation piece, mind you.

A fellow didn't meet up with a man like Slocum every day.

And now Slocum was here, investigating this whole tangled up mess. It was nigh on enough to make Foley turn tail and run.

Almost.

But then he'd have Marcus to deal with, and Marcus was a man who'd track you through hell and back just for the simple joy of shooting out your eyes, then ramming his rod up your dead ass.

Foley scraped up the last of his beans and ate them, then downed the last of his coffee. It was strong enough to stand a fork in, but he liked it that way.

Marcus always complained about the vittles on the Bar C, but they were a sight better than what Marcus cooked when they were on the trail, if you asked Foley. Course, if you asked Marcus, he'd say that Foley was the worst campfire cook in the world. And he did, at every opportunity.

Foley took his empty plate and mug back to the stove and dropped them in the pan of water at its side.

He reckoned he'd have a snort of that moonshine, if there was any left.

9

It was sometime after midnight, Slocum figured, when the moonlight shining in his face woke him from a fitful slumber.

He rolled onto his side. Pain shot up his arm to his shoulder. How come the dime novels never mentioned things like *that*?

He was getting too old for this bull. If nothing else, the damn wound would serve as a reminder to watch his back until he figured out what was going on.

Slocum stood, slipped on his pants and boots, and opened the door into the hallway.

Other than the noise coming out of Abel's room—him sawing enough cords of wood to last through the whole winter—the house was quiet.

Slocum hated to admit it, but he'd once read a dime novel or two himself. In one, the gunslinger—John Wesley Hardin or maybe Doc Holliday, he couldn't remember which—had shot some fool in the next room just for snoring.

Slocum made a bet with himself that it wasn't a tall tale.

Somewhere out on the desert, coyotes howled a tune as he quietly made his way though the house. An oil lamp, its wick turned low, burned on the fireplace mantel. Slocum tripped on one of the chairs and grabbed the back for balance.

Damn that arm! Ten years ago, he wouldn't have given a bitty little flesh wound a second thought.

The massive oak front door stood slightly ajar. He swung it open, pushed the screen, and stepped onto the veranda. He eased the door shut so that it wouldn't bang.

Slocum scanned the dark, listening for anything unusual. Nothing stirred the night air.

Glad he'd remembered to bring his tobacco pouch, he separated a rolling paper and quickly put together a smoke. Then he drew the head of a lucifer across the railing.

Dud. Spark but no fire. Just like that ruse with the slaughtered horses.

"Damn," he muttered and struck another. This time the lucifer caught and he lit the quirlie. He took a deep drag, then said, "What you doin', hidin' in the shadows, Marcus?"

"Mighty brave, don't you think?" Marcus moved into the moonlight, hand on his gun.

Slocum froze. "What do you mean?"

"For a man who nearly got his head blowed off this afternoon. Steppin' out, striking a match in the dark, no gun. Purty easy target, if someone wanted to take potshots . . . and how'd you know it was me?"

"Smelled your stink, polecat, and I don't need a gun for no varmint—"

Behind him, the screen door banged. Then he saw the glint of cold steel emerging from near his side and heard the ratchet of a hammer being cocked.

"That's right. He doesn't."

"M-Miss Miranda," Marcus stuttered in surprise. "I was just . . . just checkin' up before turning in."

"Well, now you've checked, so turn in."

Slocum flicked the butt into the yard as Marcus made his way in the direction of the bunkhouse. Slocum turned toward her voice.

Miranda stood before him, both hands barely holding up the barrel of one of his Colts. The ripe, full curves of her body showed through her wrapper. He wondered what she had on underneath.

Slocum sighed.

This was no time to go investigating. He said, "Better let me take that before you shoot somebody's foot off, darlin'."

"I was having trouble sleeping," she explained. "I heard noises—besides Uncle Abel's snoring, that is. From the front room. I went to wake you and saw you were gone, but the bed was still warm, so I figured it was you out there."

Miranda's words tripped over one another as she spoke. "Then I saw both your guns still in their holsters, and I didn't know what to think, so here I am." Her small, slender hands offered the gun, which he took.

"No more tomfoolery tonight, young lady. Back in the house with you, before you catch your death. Don't suppose Carmelita left any coffee, do you?"

He took the gun from her, slipped his free arm around her, and escorted her into the house. Slocum liked how her curves fit his body.

While Miranda rustled up a cup of coffee, Slocum stalked to his room and holstered the gun. He would not always be around to protect her.

He laughed. Just who had needed protection that time?

Remembering his saddlebags, he dug deep into them.

Having pulled something from the bottom of one, he returned to the front parlor.

Miranda was just returning from the kitchen. "What are you hiding in that big paw of yours?" She set the mug next to the lamp on the fireplace mantel and turned up the wick.

"More importantly," she purred, "what would you like to be holding?"

Slocum graced her with an easy smile and held out a single-shot derringer. "Figured if you're going to be a gunslinger, you better have a gun you can tote a mite better than my Colt."

"Oh," she cooed, taking the walnut-handled piece in her hand and aiming it at the door. "Where'd you come by something like this?" She examined the silver inlay and cross-hatched carvings.

"Took it off a saloon girl when I was kind of the temporary sheriff, right after she gut-shot some fool. The idiot didn't know enough to keep his mouth locked tight, or his pants buttoned up."

Miranda dropped the gun into her pocket and picked up the mug.

Something caught Slocum's eye. At the corner of the mantel was a collection of pipestone carvings, the red stone marbled with streaks and flecks of white. Pipes in various stages of finish and several figures of desert animals were arranged in a grouping. "Where'd these come from?"

"Been there as long as I can remember," Miranda said. "I used to play with them when I was little. Nowadays, Carmelita complains about 'em every time she has to dust." She picked up the carving of a coyote and ran her fingers over the polished stone.

"Right before he died, Papa told me he found them near the mouth of an old pipestone quarry." Miranda's voice caught.

"Pipestone quarry?" Slocum asked with arched brows. "Around here? I thought the Indians traded with the northern tribes for all their sacred stone. You're sure he said it was on this land?"

"Positive. He told me it was near the ruins, up by the waterfall. And that sometimes water covered it when the arroyos were full after a storm."

Sinuously, she draped herself on the divan. "I used to hunt for it when I'd go up there for a swim. Never found it, though. But, yes, I'm sure that's where he said it was. I wish I'd had the chance to ask—"

"What's going on out here?" Abel Cassidy shuffled into the room from the hallway.

"You're awake, Uncle Abel."

"*Course* I'm awake," he said accusingly. "Who can sleep? Goll-danged yelling, doors banging, and furniture bein' tossed all over the place. And what are you doin' out here half-nekkid?"

Slocum didn't like the way Abel leered at Miranda's figure. It was the most un-uncle-ish look he'd ever seen on a man.

Miranda appeared not to notice. "I was just showing Slocum the carvings Papa found. You know anything about 'em?"

"Nah," Abel said. Then to Slocum, he said, "My brother was a tight-lipped son of a gun. Hell, he never told me he had a safe, till right before he died. Course when I opened it, there was nothing except a stack of bills. He never was too business minded."

"And you are?" Miranda shot back. "At least my father knew enough not to bring men like Marcus and Foley around."

"What's got into you lately?" Abel bellowed. "Told you I *had* to hire them—to find out who's been feedin' my good horses to the buzzards."

"Don't you think it's a little more than strange," Miranda said with cold calm, "that nothing like that ever happened before? Not until after your pal Vance Jefferson left. Not until just before Marcus and Foley wandered in, asking for work."

"Now, don't go accusin' someone who ain't around to defend himself," Abel fairly shouted. "It was just a coincidence, an ugly coincidence."

"Seems like there've been far too many coincidences, Uncle Abel. And that's why I brought Slocum here. To make sense of those coincidences before we don't have a decent horse left on the Bar C to worry about. If I didn't know better, I'd think . . ." Miranda's voice trailed off.

Abel's voice took on a calmer but far more menacing edge. "Think what?"

Miranda grew sullen. "Nothing, Uncle Abel."

"Then go on back to bed," he snapped. "Mornin's' going to be here before we know it."

Now that was a sage bit of nothing, Slocum thought, as he headed back to his room. He punched his pillow into shape and stretched out on his back, sure he wouldn't catch another wink.

Morning came before he knew it.

It was a long night for Miranda Cassidy.

As soon as first light snaked in through her bedroom window, she was up, dressed in her pale green riding habit, and headed for the dining room. Of all the things that had happened in the past few months, mention of her father having a safe bothered her more than any of them.

She kept hearing her uncle's voice: "Hell, he never told me he had a safe, till right before he died. Course when I opened it, there was nothing except a stack of bills. He never was too business minded."

She'd never heard of any safe.

Stack of bills? Never too business minded? That was a complete pile of road apples!

Miranda plopped into a dining room chair. As if by magic, a steaming cup of coffee and a pitcher of cream appeared in front of her. "Thank you, Carmelita," she said, spooning two heaping teaspoons of sugar into the cup and adding a big dollop of cream. "Carmelita? How long have you worked on the Bar C?"

"Ever since you were a tiny thing."

"And how well did you know my father?"

Carmelita blushed, but Miranda's gaze held her fast. "*Very* well, señorita. After your *madre* die, very well."

Miranda took a sip of the steaming brew. "Did you know if my father had a safe?"

"*Sí, pequeña.*" Carmelita wiped her hands on her apron. "Your poppy say everything you need is in that safe. You didn't know?"

"I never heard a word about it until last night. Do you know where it is?"

"*Sí,* he show it to me. It is in the wall of his room, behind the painting of your mother."

"Don't mention you told me to Uncle Abel, please."

"I don't tell that *malo bastardo cabrón* nothing!" she spit out and made the sign to ward off the evil eye. Then she put an index finger to her lips and glanced toward the hallway.

• • •

Slocum strode into the dining room just in time to hear Carmelita's oath. "Mornin' ladies," he said.

"Coffee, Señor Slocum?" Carmelita greeted him with a warm smile and a twitch of her hip.

"Don't mind if I do," Slocum said, swinging his leg over a chair and hopping the chair legs up to the table. He was certain then that her words had not been for him.

"Evil bastard." That left Abel Cassidy. Well, if the shoe fit . . .

The climate sure had changed drastically since the last time he visited the Bar C.

"You drink. I bring you big breakfast," Carmelita said, and hurried off to the kitchen. Before she reached the door, she peeked over her shoulder. "How you like your eggs this morning, señor?"

"Any way you want to cook 'em. Just no salsa."

Carmelita cackled and disappeared through the door.

Slocum took in Miranda—a glorious sight, indeed. She looked awfully fine this morning. Green suited her well and the ruffles at her wrists and throat were a nice touch, he decided.

But if she was planning to go with him, he preferred the pants she had on the first time they rode to the Bar C. Slocum asked, "Feel like a jaunt this morning?"

The corners of Miranda's mouth turned up and her eyes looked downright devilish. She said in husky tones, "Depends. What you got on your mind, cowboy?"

"Thought we'd do a little exploring. Maybe see if we can find that pipestone quarry, maybe do some target practicing. You might bring that derringer along, if you've a mind to. We'll see what comes up." Slocum's voice dropped to barely a whisper. "You remember that gold piece I found on the way here?"

Miranda nodded. "Wouldn't forget something like that."

"Well now there's two."

Miranda's eyes opened wide and her jaw dropped.

"Two what?" Abel Cassidy groused, as he walked into the dining room and sat at the head of the table. He wasn't at all pleased to see that little prick tease, Miranda, talking to Slocum.

Somebody needed to teach her a lesson she wouldn't forget—and pretty damned soon. Abel was counting on being the teacher.

No, he was not pleased.

He'd expected to be long gone and out on the range before either of them cracked an eyelid.

All his careful planning. All his careful work. Everything was coming unhinged.

Now besides Marcus and Foley blackmailing him, he'd have to get rid of Slocum as well as Miranda—something he was not looking forward to tackling.

Why couldn't the little bitch have left well enough alone? She was more meddlesome than his brother had ever been.

Smarter, too.

But she was a damn sight easier on the eyes. He felt himself getting hard.

"Forgot to tell you last night, Slocum," he said, willing his erection down, "Sam Donaldson—he's our undertaker in Apache Wells—brought Dave Crone's body here for burial. Just like you asked. Said to stop off in town and he'd give you his saddle."

He paused. "Said the old codger didn't have much else. A couple of the boys put Dave up in the old cowboy cemetery and read a few Bible words over him."

"You mentioned it, Abel," Slocum said. Was the old boy getting senile, too? Either that, or his anger had erased the memory. Either way, it didn't bode well.

"I did?" Abel asked, and forced a smile. "Must be gettin' absent minded or something."

Humming, Carmelita bustled into the dining room balancing two heaping plates and a platterful of hot wheat and corn tortillas. She set one plate in front of Miranda and the other in front of Slocum, then poured Abel a mug of coffee.

"I bring your food right away, Señor Cassidy."

Abel watched Slocum tear off a chunk of corn tortilla and sop up some egg yolk before stuffing it into his mouth.

"How's that arm?"

Slocum washed his food down with a gulp of coffee before he answered. "Stiff. But it'll be fit as a fiddle in a day or two."

That arm wasn't the only stiff thing in the room. Abel shifted uncomfortably in his chair.

"Nice day for a ride," he said, making small talk. Those two had been jabbering like a couple jaybirds when he came into the room. Now they acted like they had lockjaw.

When it was clear he was not going to get anything out of them, he said, "I'll be gone most of the day. Got to see to that order for army mounts."

Carmelita's feet swished across the floor. She laid a plate of eggs, sausage, and home fries with onion in front of Abel. He guessed she was in cahoots with them, too.

Abel knew his brother had been dipping his measuring stick into her well for a long time. He should have dismissed her ass the day Judah had died. Would have if she hadn't been such a good cook.

Abel shoveled his mouth full of home fries.

"More eggs, Señor Slocum?" Carmelita asked.

"You tryin' to fatten me up?" Slocum patted her ample rump, sending Carmelita into squeals of laughter.

Abel had seen enough foolishness for one morning. He gulped down his coffee, took another bite of potato, and scooped the eggs and sausage into a couple flour tortillas to take along.

10

"What's got into him?" Slocum asked as the screen door banged behind Abel.

Miranda shrugged. "Hard to tell. But I suppose it has somethin' to do with Marcus and Foley and you and, well, everything."

"Miranda . . ." Slocum began trying to couch his words carefully. But he couldn't. So he said, "You ever stop to think that your uncle Abel might be mixed up in this thing?"

Miranda drew herself up and glared at him. "Uncle Abel? Kill his own horses? Are you crazy, Slocum?"

"There's more goin' on here than horse killin', and you know it."

"I do?"

Slocum took a deep breath to tamp his anger down. Miranda was playing dumb on purpose.

It didn't suit her.

He said, "Stop and think about it, girl. Don't it seem a coincidence that Vance Jefferson turned up on Abel's spread, followed by Marcus and Foley? Don't it seem kind of funny that the horse killin's started around then? And ain't it odd that we found a couple of double eagles just lyin' on the ground, out by the stream?"

"Yes," she admitted. "But what in the hell does one thing have to do with the others?"

"Don't know," said Slocum. "But I'm gonna find out if it's the last thing I do."

By the time they'd ridden out halfway to the canyon and the pool, Miranda had gotten over her sharpness. Apparently she had taken Slocum's theories to heart, or at least he hoped so.

By the time they were three-quarters of the way there, she was chattering like a magpie, and Slocum was happy to let her carry on. It beat the hell out of her icy silence.

He'd kept an eye open for company—namely Marcus and Foley—since they left the ranch, but so far had seen nothing.

This was good. He imagined he and Miranda had left before half the hands were all the way out of their bunks.

When they reached the little cascading stream and its pool, they ground-tied the horses and set out on foot, at Slocum's suggestion.

"Let's see if we can't find where your daddy found those carvings," he said.

Miranda cocked a brow. "If we're gonna do something totally unrelated to any of the problems at hand, I think we oughta take advantage of the pool. If you know what I mean. And I'm sure you do."

Slocum grinned. "Let's play hide-and-seek for the pipe-stone first, and then the other, all right?"

Miranda shrugged, and set off up the hill, climbing carefully.

Slocum followed, although he wasn't entirely certain she was going in the right direction. She acted as if she'd climbed this rise a dozen times before—at least, she seemed certain where all the handholds and footholds were—but he wanted to explore new territory.

Still, he followed her up her familiar path. But then, about halfway up, something caught his eye. It was the narrow shadow of a concavity some fifteen feet to the side, and he began to work his way over to it.

Miranda happened to glance back, and she hollered, "Hey! Where you going?"

"You ever been over this way?" he shouted back.

She climbed down a few steps, then began to sidle across the rock wall after him.

At last, he reached the shadow, which turned into a narrow slit in the rock face. He popped a lucifer with his thumbnail and held it inside the cave.

No critters anyway. But the rock showed streaks of red-and-white marbled rock.

Pipestone, in Arizona!

"I'll be double damned," he muttered.

"Probably," said Miranda, from behind him. "Are you going to tell me what's in there or not?"

"The source of your daddy's trinkets," he said, and shook out the lucifer. It was burning his fingers. "Outcrop of pipestone."

"Can we get inside?" she asked eagerly.

"Reckon." He flicked another lucifer to life, held it out ahead of him, sucked in his stomach, and squeezed through the opening. Then he held his hand out to Miranda, who slipped through the opening with no problem.

Her hand went immediately to the streaked stone of the wall. "You're right!" she said.

He grinned. "You don't have to act so surprised about it. I usually am, you now."

"I didn't mean . . . Oh, you!" she said, and playfully pushed against his chest.

Slocum could see where men, long ago, had chopped stone from the walls, sometimes roughly, sometimes delicately. The cave was barely tall enough for him to stand in, and about ten feet deep.

There were areas where the digging went back several feet into the rock, others where it went back only a few inches, and some where stone seemed to have been sheared off even with the walls.

But there was no time for further investigation, because Miranda was pulling at his sleeve. "All right, we found daddy's pipestone. Can we visit the pool now, Slocum? My clothes are all . . . itchy."

"Oh? Itchy, are they?" he said as he shook out his match, leaving them in darkness, save for the crescent of light that came in through the opening. He wondered if thousands of years ago, the pipestone had presented itself to the outside face of the wall, and if this little cave hadn't been slowly mined and dug out, following the ore over many years.

"Itchy," he repeated. "Well, we can't have that, can we?"

He started to take her in his arms, but she was too quick for him. She darted out the opening and was making her way down the hillside before he could collect himself. He peeked out. She was making good time, too.

She beamed up at him. "Footholds! Somebody carved footholds in here!"

"Not surprised," he said as he squeezed back out into the sunshine. If the Indians—Apache and Navajo, most likely, or maybe Pima, Maricopa, or Hohokam—had used this place to quarry pipestone, they naturally would have wanted to make the frequent climb easier.

He carefully followed her down the hill, but the footholds weren't made for big American feet wearing bigger American boots, and he slipped and slid as much as climbed down.

"Very smooth, Slocum," she said with a grin when he finally made it down to the flat.

"Big feet," he said, returning her smile.

"I've heard that about you. You know, big feet, big . . . other things . . ."

He suddenly swept her up and carried her, laughing, over to the flat rock where they'd spent time the other morning. He set her on her feet, saying, "All right, girl, now you're askin' for it," and proceeded to unbutton her bodice.

She responded by going to work on the buttons of his shirt. "I thought you'd *never* get to this, Slocum!" she breathed.

He paused his fingers. "Well, if you want to go looking for another cave, I'll be glad to—"

"Shut up!" she said, laughing, and pulled his shirt off.

He had reached the end of the buttons on her bodice, but he'd be damned if he could figure out how the rest of the contraption worked. So he simply pulled apart the layers of undergarments covering her breasts to bare them, and latched his mouth to a ripe nipple. He supposed all the clothes this morning were in response to her uncle's comment the night before.

He needn't have worried about the rest of her garments, though. She peeled out of them faster than he could peel a banana, and was suddenly, wonderfully naked in his arms.

He lowered his mouth to her willing lips and drank of her sweetness while she fumbled with his gunbelt, then his trousers. Both fell into a pool around his ankles. He was hard as a rock and ready to go, but he broke off the kiss and said, "Boots, honey."

She rolled her eyes, but waited while he sat down. She took one of his boots between her legs, and he pushed on her fanny with the other, then repeated the action with the other foot until both boots were off. He shook off his britches, then stood and took her hand.

"I hate that part," she muttered.

"But I love it, baby," he said, grinning smugly. "Nothin' in the world like my boot on a pretty gal's bare backside."

She gave his arm a slap, but was careful to avoid the wounded area, which was healing nicely. "Men are pigs," she said.

"But I notice that you're here—and naked—with one of us," he said, cupping her cheek and running a thumb lightly over her lips. "We can't be *all* bad."

"I will admit, some of you are *sightly* better than others." She stepped into the pool and pulled him along with her, a willing captive.

She sank down on the smooth sandstone floor of the pool, the water coming just up to her shoulders, and snaked her arms up his chest, letting her hands wander over his scars, comb his chest hair. He was happy to note that the water was pleasantly warm and had done nothing to dampen his . . . enthusiasm.

In any way, shape, or form.

He drew her close and kissed her long and deep, then slid his hands down her long, sleek back to cup her ripe buttocks in both hands.

He lifted her, the water helping to buoy her up, while she spread her legs, wrapping them around him, embracing him.

He eased her down on his cock until he was fully enveloped in her. Smooth, hot, and slippery, she was, and very enthusiastic.

She wrapped her arms about his neck and, slowing, began to move up and down, swirling, dancing on him sensuously.

He moved with her, keeping a precarious balance for the both of them on the stone edge of the pool, rising and falling, dancing and weaving, grinding and releasing.

Slowly, their tempo grew faster, their sighs turned to pants, their lovemaking became rougher, and each sensation grew sharper, more intense.

And then Slocum felt Miranda explode, and he stilled himself, holding her quivering body until she quieted, before he began again. This time, he pounded vigorously up into her little body while she held on tight, whispering, "Yes, yes, yes!"

This time, they came as one, while she called his name and he bucked into her a last time.

Later, they sat, half-dressed, at the side of the pool. Slocum's arm was around Miranda, and her head was on his shoulder. "I wish every day could be like this," she said idly.

"Be nice," Slocum said.

She turned her head to face him. "Why can't it? Why can't you stay on, Slocum?"

His mouth quirked up in a little smile, and he gave her nose a pinch. "You know better than that, Miranda."

"I suppose I do. But still . . ."

She was still naked from the waist up, and Slocum cupped one breast, stroking the nipple with his thumb until it beaded.

"You're a beautiful gal, Miranda, and someday, you're going to have this whole place in your name. You won't have any trouble attractin' a better man than me. One that'll stick around. I promise."

She snorted softly, then said, "Slocum, something rather odd happened. Last night, Uncle Abel mentioned my daddy's safe."

"Yeah, I remember. So?"

"So I didn't know anything about it. Uncle Abel said it was full of unpaid bills, but Carmelita said Daddy told her it had 'everything I'd ever need' in it. Frankly, I think I trust Carmelita more than Uncle Abel."

Slocum frowned. "And you never heard anything about this safe before?"

She shook her head. "I'm telling you, I didn't know he even had one. Carmelita says it's in the wall of his room, behind my mama's portrait. I mean, don't you think that's strange? That he never mentioned it to me, I mean?"

"Yes, I do," Slocum replied, and slid his hand away from her breast. "Get dressed, honey. I think it's time to go back to the old homestead."

She heaved a small sigh. "If you say so. But I'm going under protest."

He grinned. "Noted."

11

The ride back seemed shorter.

Her body still tingling from the encounter at the pool, Miranda's thoughts came into focus on the facts. Money had been tight since her father died. Mainly, she decided, due to Uncle Abel's penchant for faro, not because of unpaid bills.

Fiction. All of it. Maybe the answers were still in that safe.

Much as she hated to admit it, Slocum was probably right. Truth was, she wouldn't put anything past her uncle. She was young when her father died, and no one had ever told her how it happened. Just that he'd fallen from his horse and hit his head. Papa had never regained consciousness.

Again, she asked herself how this could be possible. Her father had been known—and justifiably so—as the toughest bronc rider around. How in the world had Bertha, his trusty old saddle horse, thrown him?

And Uncle Abel had been with him when it happened.

Lately, he had made her skin crawl. Not that he'd done

anything out of line. Mostly the sly looks when he thought she wasn't looking. And remarks that often held a double meaning.

"Penny for your thoughts," Slocum said, pulling Cougar up next to her. "You been awful quiet on the way back."

"Just thinking," she replied as the trail rounded an out-cropping of rock. Then she heard a *zip, zip,* followed immediately by gunshots echoing off the hillsides.

"Back," Slocum yelled.

They wheeled the horses and ducked behind the rocks.

It was a bone-chilling sound. Slocum hadn't heard bullets flying that close—and missing—since the war. In an instant, he was off Cougar and catching Miranda as she slid to the ground. He threw her down and drew his revolvers. Several more shots pinged against the rocks, showering them with chips.

Cross fire!

Slocum grabbed Miranda's arm and pushed her into a crevice. He wedged himself in behind her. Cougar stood about ten feet off to the side, his normally white-ringed eyes showing red and his ears pinned.

But Miranda's horse bucked, and then reared before racing toward the Bar C.

And then he heard Miranda moan. Two more shots slammed into the dirt a few feet away. Slocum emptied one of his Colts toward a grove of cottonwoods. More than one person seemed to be firing. A flash and another chunk of rock was blown off beside his ear.

Behind him, Miranda choked out a scream. He pushed tightly against her. From the corner of his eye, Slocum saw movement. And a red checkered shirt, suspiciously like the one Abel Cassidy had worn that morning. Another bullet whizzed overhead.

Slocum sighted and got off another shot. Then all was quiet.

"Are they gone?" Miranda whispered after a long moment.

"Hush, baby." Slocum removed his hat and crouched to pick up a stick. He placed his hat on the tip and slowly inched it out of the crevice. Nothing. "Seems so."

"Did you see who it was?"

Slocum gingerly eased himself out and scanned the terrain. "Didn't get a clear sight, but I can guess."

"Why would anyone try to kill us?" she asked.

"Those shots were just scare tactics. Out there in the open, we were like ducks on a pond. Come on out. Seems safe enough now."

She didn't move.

Slocum turned and began to pull her up and out. "You stuck in there, or—"

Miranda's hand covered the right side of her face. Blood oozed between her fingers. Her eyes rolled back in her head and then closed. He caught her before she slumped to the ground.

Slocum bent over her, too stunned to move.

Don't panic, he thought. *Stay calm and just think.* But a cry broke from his lips. "Miranda!"

She didn't answer, but the pulse in the hollow of her throat beat a strong rhythm. There was an ugly bruise forming above her eye. Blood streamed from a small cut.

Must have been struck by a rock fragment, he decided. *Bastards!*

Slocum whistled and Cougar moved in close. The trusty

Appaloosa would shield them from view if those rotten sonsabitches were still out there.

He reached for his canteen. The water was still cool. Slocum removed his bandanna and soaked it. Then, wringing it out, he squatted and gently wiped Miranda's face.

Her eyelids fluttered. "Wh-what happened?" She tried to sit, but collapsed again. She groaned weakly and closed her eyes. "My head."

"Don't worry, honey. You're fine. Just a little scratch."

Slocum spoke calmly, but inside his blood was boiling. Someone would pay dearly for this. If he had his way, they wouldn't die an easy death, either. "You lay still. I'll be right back."

"Don't go," she cried.

"Miranda, you can't ride. Besides, your horse ran off. Now be a good girl and listen."

Slocum rinsed the cloth, folded it, and placed it over her eyes. "Just rest a minute. I'll be back before you know it."

Slocum stood and covered the open ground to the cottonwoods. Whoever had hid in the trees had been there awhile. Their horses had cropped the grass and trampled the ground where they had been tethered. The shooters' rock-lined fire ring still smoked.

He kicked the ashes. Beneath them, embers still glowed. Scattered around the campsite were remnants of the bushwhackers' meal.

Drawing his knife, Slocum quickly hacked down two long poles and dragged them to the rock formation where Miranda waited. She appeared to be sleeping, but as he approached, he saw her draw a bead on him with the little one-shot derringer he'd given her.

"Miranda. Put that thing down. It's me."

Slocum untied his pack roll and lashed the blanket to

the poles in a makeshift travois. Then he rigged the carrier to Cougar's saddle and strapped it into place.

Miranda's wound had stopped bleeding, but it looked terrible. He traced the edges of the bruise with his fingertips, then probed her forehead for signs her skull was broken.

Thankfully, like most of the scalp wounds he'd seen, it looked worse than it actually was. Miranda would have one mountain of a headache, though.

"This isn't gonna be a fun ride," he told her, lifting her onto the travois. "But easier than me tryin' to hold onto you while Cougar carries the both of us back to the ranch. We're still a few miles out."

There was no guesswork to it. Miranda was in terrible pain and faded in and out of consciousness. She grimaced and slipped the derringer into her pocket, though. All the fight seemed to flow out of her as he secured her to the carrier.

"Whatever you say," she murmured. "I'll try to be brave," she added, just before she passed out again.

And brave she was, Slocum thought, leading Cougar during Miranda's bone-jarring trek to the ranch. "I'm right proud of you," he told her more than once as she slipped in and out of her senses.

Slocum hatched several plans on the way back. If he told Abel she was dead, he'd want to see the body. But if he let Abel think she'd escaped with only a minor wound, Miranda would be in danger anytime he left her alone to track the rest of those bushwhackers.

And he couldn't very well tip his hand too soon, or they'd be long gone before he caught them.

Shit!

Kicking a rock in frustration, he kept walking.

Long shadows hugged the ground as they approached the Bar C's outbuildings. Miranda groaned with each jounce and jolt.

Rage and little else filled Slocum's brain. Only concern for her safety prevented him from lighting out after those bastards right then and there, catching them and killing them on the spot. Trial be damned.

They'd admitted to killing Dave Crone. *Accident my ass*. And now Miranda. Pure luck and poor aim had prevented her from being dead, too.

He wished he'd listened closer to Dave's stories about Yaqui tortures. Like the dime novels said, shooting was too good for those bastards.

He stopped short of the main house. Near an old tack shed, he untied Miranda from the travois.

She opened her eyes. "This isn't the house."

"Just trust me awhile longer," he said, helping her into the shed. He swept tack and tools off a workbench and helped Miranda up.

Covering her with the blanket, he told her, "Wait here and don't make any noise." Then he tossed the travois inside and smoothed out its telltale tracks.

Slocum rode Cougar to the front of the house. "Carmelita," he yelled, without dismounting.

Abel Cassidy banged open the screen and rushed onto the veranda. Evil surrounded him. And he was still wearing that damned red shirt. "What the hell have you done with my niece?" he shouted.

"I thought she was here," Slocum answered.

"Why the blazes would I ask where she was, if she was here?" he said.

"Calm down, Abel," Slocum said, feeling anything but calm himself.

"Bandits attacked us," he went on. "Probably the same lot that's been killin' the horses. I chased 'em off, but Miranda was hoppin' mad at me for not killin' them outright. She took off. Told me not to follow her. I figured she came back here, and now you're sayin' you ain't seen her?"

Slocum didn't have to work hard at putting a worried look on his face. And if he did say so himself, he was a damn good liar.

"Christ on a crutch! No, she ain't here," Abel bellowed, his face turning red. "Are you thick-headed or somethin'? That damned horse of hers came back two hours ago, all in a lather and winded. Musta threw her out there someplace."

"Pipe down, Abel," Slocum said. "She'll be back when she gets good and cold, which oughta be pretty damned soon. Till then, I'm stabling Cougar and then getting me somethin' to eat. I'm hungry as a grizzly bear in spring."

Abel trailed him to the horse barn. "If anything's happened to my niece, I'm holdin' you personally responsible."

It was all Slocum could do to stay composed. For once, he felt like behaving worse than any melodrama those dime novel hack writers could dream up.

Instead he said, "All right. Soon as I grab a bite, I'll go back up the trail and look. Why don't you saddle your horse and start without me?"

It was already twilight.

Certain Cassidy was out of earshot, Slocum ran to the tack shed. As soon as he opened the door, Miranda threw herself into his arms. "Slocum."

"Glad to see you up and about." He could tell she'd worked herself into a mighty rage all by herself. "Let's get something to eat and see if we can come up with a plan."

Slocum half carried, half dragged Miranda to the back door of the house.

Carmelita was throwing a dishpan full of water on the rosebushes. She tossed the pan aside and came running.

"¡Madre de Dios! Miranda! Slocum! What happen? You worry Carmelita sick." She looped one of Miranda's arms around her shoulders and helped Slocum take her into the kitchen.

Carmelita scurried between the stove and table while Miranda and Slocum filled her in with details of the ambush and Carmelita intermittently fussed over Miranda's bruised face.

Slocum helped himself to another piece of chicken fried steak and cornbread as Carmelita refilled his cup. He said, "So that leaves us with a big problem. What to do with Miranda while I find out the truth."

A big grin split Carmelita's face. "Señor Cassidy and those hombres look all over the range and desert, yes?"

"Yes," Slocum said. "And they won't give up till they find her."

"Carmelita tell you one place they never think to look. You come with me."

Miranda looked a whole lot better after her meal, Slocum thought. Still, he slipped his arm around her waist and followed Carmelita down the hall toward the bedrooms. Then she paused in front of Miranda's father's door.

"In here," Carmelita said, unlocking the door with a key from the ring on her belt. "Your uncle, he never come in here. He's afraid of this room. He think it's haunted."

12

Miranda slept fitfully on her father's wide bed, the one he'd shared with her mother all those years ago.

She must have had fever dreams, because she was certain that someone came and sat on the side of the mattress beside her and soothed her head with long, lean fingers. And in her dream, she was certain that that someone was her father.

"It's all right, girl," he whispered, in her head. "You're gonna be just fine, my darlin'."

But when she forced herself to fully come awake, there was no one there.

She thought on this for a time, then softly smiled. "Papa, you do still look over me, don't you?"

She felt a good deal better than she had, although her face still stung and her head still thudded. She discovered she could stand unaided. Her gaze traveled over the room and its contents, things she hadn't seen for years. Not since her uncle Abel ordered the room locked up.

There was Mama's dressing set: silver, inset with

mother-of-pearl. Her Papa had never put it away. He said it gave him comfort, as if she might be coming back. They had been so much in love, those two.

Miranda found that just being in the room again had brought silent tears to her eyes, and she rubbed them away with the back of her hand.

This wasn't the time for tears. It was the time for a little snooping.

She crossed the room to the oil portrait of her mother, painted when Mama was a young woman, before she had married Papa and come west with him. She looked lovely, seated on a park bench in her old-fashioned clothes and wonderful pearls and holding a parasol, amid banks and banks of blooming flowers and trees. She'd had red hair, like Miranda.

Miranda eased the heavy frame away from the wall, to one side. There was the safe, all right.

Miranda tried to open it, but it was locked. Little scratches—and a few gouges—etched the metal around the dial and the handle, and when she looked more closely, the edges of the door. Someone had tried to force his way into the safe, apparently to no avail.

Uncle Abel was the first—and only—name that sprang to mind.

She attempted to open it herself. She tried her father's birthday, her mother's birthday, and her birthday, but not one combination worked. Sighing, she let the portrait swing gently back into place, and began to search for the combination.

Her daddy hadn't been a slipshod kind of man, not like his brother Abel could be. He would have written that combination down someplace!

•   •   •

Slocum set out on Abel's trail. Not that there was much to see, but at least he had a general direction to follow, and the moon was nearly full in an almost cloudless sky.

At least Cougar had had a chance to eat, and he'd had a break. He was fresh as a daisy.

Slocum moved at a walk or a slow jog-trot, keeping his eyes open for any sign of movement that was out of the ordinary. He'd checked the bunkhouse before he'd gone into the barn. The man reported that Marcus and Foley hadn't yet come in, and when he got to the barn, their horses weren't there.

It was a pretty safe bet they wouldn't be coming in at all. And he was beginning to think that Abel wouldn't be, either. Probably end up camped somewhere with those two owlhoots, once he figured out he wasn't going to find Miranda.

And then he heard it: somebody shouting, "Miranda! Miranda, girl!"

Abel. It was pretty far off, but the land here was flat for miles, and sound carried. Slocum started off toward the calls, his hand on the butt of his gun.

Miranda sorted through her father's chest of drawers, then her mother's, looking for a scrap of paper. Anything with numbers on it!

But no. Nothing. She went through her mother's dressing table, drawer by drawer, carefully replacing all the contents just so—and once stopping to dab on a bit of her mother's perfume.

It was heavenly!

That done with no results, she went to the tall chifforobe in the corner and gave it the same treatment she had given the bureaus.

Nothing! Just a few dresses and her father's old duster. She'd gone through the pockets of that, too.

Dejected, she sat down on the bed, her face in her hands. "Where'd you put it, Papa?" she whispered. "Where on earth?"

And then, almost miraculously, she had an idea. She rushed to her mother's dressing table once more, pulled the center drawer all the way out, and dumped its contents on the top.

There, taped to the bottom of the drawer, was the combination. Or *a* combination, anyway.

Miranda struck her forehead with her knuckles, and was immediately sorry. It took her a moment to regain her former clarity, but when she did, she was up and headed for her mother's portrait.

This time, she put the drawer down, bottom side up, in the chair beneath the painting, and once again moved the frame to one side. With trembling fingers, she moved the tumblers in the fading light, and heard a soft, satisfying click with each one.

When she pulled on the handle, the door swung easily outward. She gasped, and put a hand over her mouth. It was just like in a play or a book, wasn't it? What would she find?

She rigged the open safe door to hold the painting to one side, then picked up a candle and held it close to the safe's dark interior.

Papers. A smallish needlework bag. A few more of those pipestone pieces. That was all, and her grin faded. But she removed everything, closed the safe, and righted the picture.

Then she carried her plunder to the bed, where she could look it over at her leisure.

• • •

Abel Cassidy had ridden a big loop in his search for his niece, but he wasn't going to find her. Not tonight. It crossed his mind that she might have straggled into the Bar C already.

Maybe she'd need a little . . . comforting.

That thought got him halfway hard, and he grinned. Yes sir, she just might.

He headed back toward the ranch, going a different way than he had come. In fact, it was much the same route he'd taken the night he killed Miranda's father.

They said it was a terrible thing to kill your brother, but when your brother has everything—including a fine ranch and an even finer daughter—and you have nothing, then sometimes it's justified.

At least, that's what he'd been telling himself all these years. He pretty much believed it by this time, too.

He had bounced a rock off his brother's temple just as hard as he could, and he was dead—and Abel was a landowner—just like that. Easy as pie.

No, easier. He could never figure out why they said that pie was easy. Damn hard to make, if you asked him! All that nonsense with crusts . . .

At last, the Bar C came into dim view, and grew closer and clearer with every step of his horse. Pretty soon he'd be home. And Miranda, that curvaceous little minx, would be waiting for him.

Probably be tired after her long walk, too. Wouldn't put up too much of a fight . . .

After he had his way with her, he'd put her out of the picture. Permanently.

Tomorrow, he'd take care of Slocum, too. He wouldn't be a bit surprised if the big man wasn't hanging around

Miranda for the same reason. He just wanted to get under her petticoats, that was all. Well, Abel would be damned if he'd let that happen!

He'd kill Slocum, all right, then arrange everything to look like Miranda had killed him while he was raping her at gunpoint. And of course, Slocum's gun had gone off with the blast of her shot.

Very clever. Very clever indeed.

He gained the yard, dismounted, and led his horse into the barn.

Miranda's eyes had grown as round as saucers when she read her father's will.

This place had never belonged to Uncle Abel at all, either in whole or in part! It had been her papa's, and he had left the whole thing—buildings, livestock, and all—to her!

How could Uncle Abel lie like he had?

What nerve!

What unmitigated gall!

What a shitheel.

By the time she finished reading, she was trembling. She'd show him! Tomorrow, she'd fire Marcus and Foley, and fire Uncle Abel's ass, too. She was willing to bet that their absence would put a quick stop to the horse killings.

She hadn't gotten to the needlework bag yet, but she was so thirsty. Maybe finding out you're rich did that to a person. Well, finding out you have property, anyway. Uncle Abel had never done much more than break even on the ranch.

But then, she didn't play cards! She wouldn't be throwing money away by bucking the tiger's odds!

She went to the door, opened it, and called softly, "Carmelita? Could I have a glass of lemonade, please?"

There was a pause before Carmelita answered, rather stiffly, "In a moment."

"Thank you," Miranda replied, and closed the door again, wondering who had put the burr up Carmelita's bustle.

She had just reached the bed again and was starting to reach for the mysterious bag, when she heard footsteps approaching. Not Carmelita's, though. Carmelita didn't wear spurs—or boots—or walk with such a heavy tread.

Slocum? No, he was out—

The door abruptly swung in. Abel Cassidy stood in the doorway, his eyes sweeping over Miranda, the papers, the bag, then flicking toward the painting. The upside-down drawer still sat in the chair beneath it.

His expression altered for the worse.

"You found the combination, didn't you, you little bitch?"

"Uncle Abel—"

"After I turned this whole place upside down and sideways, you found it!"

"Yes." Miranda swung her legs off the bed and faced him. "This is *my* ranch Uncle Abel. Mine. All mine, lock stock, and barrel."

"*All mine, all mine,*" he parroted cruelly.

"You shut up!" she snapped.

"No, you," he said, taking a step into the room and shoving her down, flat on her back. And on the bag from the safe.

He forced apart her knees with his and began to unbutton his britches. "Fine," he said as he yanked her skirts up to her waist, "take your stupid ranch for the time being. But after tonight, you're gonna be mine—and then you're gonna be dead!"

Miranda tried to twist away, but his legs between hers and his hand on her chest held her prisoner. And then he dug his gnarly old fingers into the material of her bodice and ripped it away.

"You pig!" she shouted. "Leave me alone! Carmelita, help!"

He bent, lowering his torso near. "Oh, she can't hear you, girl. Or if she can, she can't do nothin' about it. I left her tied up on the cold-keep porch." He smiled. "Ain't nobody comin' to help poor little Miranda."

And she felt his hand between her legs, moving material aside.

"Don't you dare!" she spat.

"Oh, I dare. I dare plenty."

She raked her nails down his face, but it didn't faze him. She knew if he was that bent on doing her mischief, she only had one recourse.

"One thing first, Abel," she said, fishing frantically in her pocket.

He squinted. "What?"

"That night. When you led my papa's horse in with him across the saddle . . ." Her fingers found what she sought, and she brought it out, hidden first by the material of her skirts, then the bedding. "Did you kill him?"

Abel had the nerve to smile. "That's for me to know and you to find out, doll-baby. Now look out, I'm a-gonna kiss you!"

His head lowered, only to meet Miranda's derringer. He just had time to look a little surprised before she pulled the trigger.

Slocum had lost Abel: He finally had to admit it. And now clouds had moved across the sky to cover the moon.

He was out of luck.

He climbed down off Cougar to take a long, satisfying piss against a barrel cactus, and Cougar responded by taking a piss of his own.

He poured water from his canteen into his cupped palm, and the gelding drank, then Slocum repeated the process until there was no water left.

"That's it, old son," he said, patting the gelding's neck. "The well's gone dry."

Cougar snorted, as if he objected to this oversight on Slocum's part, and Slocum said, "Don't blame you. Guess we're gonna have to find our way back to the ranch by feel."

13

Miranda pried Abel's corpse off and slithered out from under him and off the bed. She was filled with conflicting emotions, among them rage, hurt, sorrow, umbrage, and horror. But most of all, rage.

She ran to her own room to grab a robe, then ran to the kitchen and out to the cold-keep porch. Carmelita sat on the floor, bound hand and foot, trying to saw through her ropes—without much luck—with a corner of a shelf filled with jelly jars.

When she saw Miranda coming, she said, "Thank the Lord! Are you—"

And then she took in Miranda's hastily donned robe, and the torn dress sticking out from beneath it. *"Madre de Dios,"* Carmelita wept as Miranda cut the ropes from her hands and feet. "What did he do? What has happened? I heard a shot!"

Instinctively, Miranda channeled her own burgeoning hysteria into something useful—getting Carmelita calmed down.

She helped the older woman to her feet, saying, "It's all right now, Carmelita. It could have been really bad, but it's all right. I took care of it."

She took Carmelita out through the kitchen to the parlor, and sat next to her on the couch, enfolding the older woman's shoulders in her arms.

"But what happen?" Carmelita continued, her head twisting like a nervous hen's. "Where is your uncle? What was that shot? I hope he was not shooting in the house again! The last time, he murdered my best figure of Our Lady of Guadalupe!"

Miranda opened her mouth to explain, but just then someone started banging on the front door. "Come in!" she shouted.

The latch jiggled, followed by a call of "It's locked!"

Miranda recognized the voice. It was Berto Rodriguez, one of the Bar C's older hands. She called, "Just a minute, Berto," and stood up, patting Carmelita's shoulder. "I'll be right back," she whispered.

Berto practically fell in on her when she unlocked the door.

"Sorry, Miss Miranda, ma'am," he said while he regained his balance. "We thought we heard a shot, out at the bunkhouse, I mean. Just wanted to make sure everything was all right . . ."

His eyes slid down to her chest, and Miranda pulled her robe tighter. However, the thin garment couldn't disguise the bunched and ripped fabric beneath.

"Berto," she said, getting him to focus on her face again, "I'm afraid I've killed Uncle Abel. The body's down the hall, in my papa's old room."

She offered no further information, just sat down next to Carmelita once more, and comforted her.

"B-but, Miss Miranda!" Berto stammered. "What the hell happened? I mean heck. Jesus Christ! Abel's dead?"

Berto was getting himself worked up into quite a state, and Miranda finally shouted, "Alberto!" When he quieted, she went on, "Berto, it's all right, now. He tried to . . . force himself on me, and I had no recourse but to shoot him."

"*Es verdad,*" added Carmelita shakily. "He come in the house and tie me up like he knew what he was going to do to Miss Miranda. He had the face of *el Diablo* himself! I never see him look like that before!" She crossed herself, bowed her head, and began to mumble a prayer in Spanish.

"You shot him dead, Miss Miranda?" asked Berto, who apparently couldn't quite grasp the situation. "All the way dead? Are you sure?"

"Yes, Berto," she said, weary of the whole ordeal, and growing a little dulled to it, too. "He's as dead as a hammer, I'm afraid. Go and take a look."

At last he stomped down the hall. Miranda listened to his bootsteps as he turned into her father's room, and then heard Berto's exclamation of "*¡Madre de Dios!* Right between the eyes!"

Well, Berto always was one to be a bit theatrical.

She felt Carmelita's arm come round her shoulders, and realized that the dynamics of the situation had changed.

Carmelita hugged her and whispered, "You are very brave, so very brave. He was the pig, *el puerco!* My poor, poor baby. I bring you a brandy, yes?"

As Carmelita stood up, Miranda said, "Get one for yourself, too, Carmelita."

They both deserved a stiff belt.

● ● ●

Slocum moved slowly, taking advantage of the infrequent break in the cover of clouds to speed up, but mostly he let Cougar just plod along at his own pace.

The bad thing was that Abel would come back to the Bar C in the morning, and they'd have to stall him again about Miranda. But the good thing, he thought, smiling to himself, was that she was waiting for him back at the ranch.

There was good and bad in everything.

When the clouds finally moved past the moon again, he nearly broke into song. He nudged Cougar into a soft jog, and the gelding leapt at the chance to speed up a little. Slocum rounded a bend—and ran right into Marcus and Foley's camp.

Both of them brought their guns up directly, and Slocum was so downright surprised to find them there that he reined in Cougar and just sat in the saddle, speechless.

But he recovered himself in a moment, and said, "You boys draw on everybody who rides up on you, or is this special, just for me?"

Foley smirked, but holstered his gun. Marcus, Slocum noted, was a little slower to respond. But he holstered his gun, just the same.

Slocum said, "Mind if I step down and have a cupa coffee?" There was a pot sitting on the edge of their small fire.

"No skin off my back," growled Foley.

"Only if you got your own cup," snarled Marcus. "We don't carry no tea sets for company."

Slocum forced himself to keep a straight face, and said, "Yeah, I got my own."

He swung down and dug through his saddlebag for his tin cup, then knelt beside the fire and poured himself a mugful.

"And don't go askin' for no cream nor sugar," snapped Foley.

It was all Slocum could do to keep from laughing out loud. Foley had missed his true calling—he really ought to go on the stage.

Slocum sat on his heels and sipped at the brew. It was pretty bad, but better than nothing for a man who'd been wandering in the dark for a few hours and had given the last of his water to his horse.

"Right good," he lied, keeping his eyes on both of them.

"It's liquid horseshit and you know it," remarked Marcus. "Foley never could make decent coffee. Or anything else, for that matter."

Slocum had just noticed something decidedly odd about Foley's shirt, and asked, "What'd you tussle with, Foley? Looks like you tore your sleeve up good."

Foley didn't answer, but Marcus barked out a laugh and said, "He tangled with a badger! Damn near took his arm off, too. Would have, if I hadn't shot it."

Now, how in the world a badger had managed to get from the ground and clear up on Foley's arm—while Foley was probably on horseback, to boot—was a puzzlement.

Slocum said, "You boys got flyin' badgers around here? Anything I should be worried about?"

Foley snapped, "Don't be a fool, Slocum! It done attacked me on the ground!"

"He had his arm up the den at the time," Marcus said, and laughed again.

Foley with his arm up a badger den? This time, Slocum couldn't hold back his laughter.

"What the hell were you doin' that for?" he asked, once he caught his breath. "You were just askin' for it, Foley."

He watched as a warning look flickered over Marcus's face, directed at Foley, and then Foley's expression changed.

Foley turned to Slocum and said, "Just cause you laughed, I ain't a-gonna tell you. So there." He looked back at Marcus, who sent him a nod, as if he'd done the right thing.

"You stayin' all night, Slocum?" Marcus asked curtly.

Slocum tossed back the last of his bad coffee, then stood up. "As appealin' as you make it sound, Marcus, I believe I'll be off before we turn this into a slumber party. Appreciate the coffee, though."

With that, he stepped back up on Cougar, tucked his mug down into his saddlebag again, and reined away from the fire.

Nobody said good-bye.

Slocum didn't expect them to.

Actually, he half-expected a slug in his back, but it appeared that these boys weren't going to be so bold at the moment. Slocum figured that there weren't any trees for them to hide behind, and chuckled softly.

The moon had come out again, and looked like it was going to remain free of cloud cover for a good time, so Slocum had no qualms about setting Cougar off in a jog. He could see pretty well, and the ground was flat.

He couldn't help but wonder, though, how in the heck Foley had managed to get his arm clear up a badger's den—and why! He could think of a thousand other things he'd rather do for sport.

He also wondered why he hadn't run across Abel, or any sign of him. Frankly, when he'd first stumbled into Marcus and Foley's camp, he'd half-expected Abel Cassidy to stand up from the shadows with his rifle raised.

But then thoughts of Miranda wiped the badger's den—and Abel—from his mind.

He jogged on, toward the ranch, with a smile on his lips.

• • •

Berto had fetched Dilly, another trusted hand, and swearing an oath not to tell a living soul, the two of them had moved Uncle Abel's body to his own room until the morning, when they would bury him.

But Miranda still had to go back to the scene of her ordeal—and his death. There were the papers to retrieve, and the bag, and the little pipestone pieces to be gathered up.

The papers had Uncle Abel's blood on them, and she set them aside on her nightstand to dry. And hopefully, the blood would magically vanish. She could dream, couldn't she?

She sat down on her bed and spread out the pipestone pieces, but couldn't make heads or tails of them. The bag she pulled onto her lap and opened.

She didn't move for quite a while. She couldn't take her eyes off its contents.

Finally, gingerly, lest it evaporate as she was wishing Abel's blood would, she reached inside.

Money.

Good, honest, American scrip.

Bundles and bundles of it!

She began to count it out, her eyes twinkling while a smile danced around the corners of her mouth.

Marcus was filling the coffeepot this time. He could put up with a lot from Foley, but one pot of his stinking coffee was all he could stand.

He set the pot on the fire, then leaned back. Things weren't going very well. First, they'd had to kill Jefferson, then Crone—well that had been an accident, sort of—and now it looked like they'd have to take out Slocum, too.

He didn't know that he was up to plugging Slocum, not

unless they caught him out in the open with his back turned
again.

Back in the old days, Slocum had been nothing but solid
speed with a gun, and if a man listened to the stories going
around, he had only gotten faster with the passage of years.

Marcus sure knew that Foley couldn't do it. Not a
prayer of it from close up and certainly not from the distance Marcus planned. There was no way either of them
would face off with Slocum!

Plus, they were going to have to stop killing horses
pretty soon. Abel was making some awful strong sounds
about it.

Well, to be honest, threats. When they'd killed that good
roping horse of his, he'd nearly busted a blood vessel.

Well, how was Marcus to know it was a good horse? It
looked just like all the others out there on the range.

A horse was a horse was a horse, so far as he was concerned.

And they were no closer to the stash than they'd been
when they arrived at the Bar C. Foley was getting so desperate that early this evening, he'd stuck his arm clear up
to the elbow into a hole he thought might be a hiding place.
He yanked that arm out fast, though, when he touched hair
instead of gold, and that badger came ripping out right
along with him.

It was plenty riled, too.

But Marcus had shot it, saving both Foley's arm and
gaining them supper at the same time.

He started to chuckle again, thinking about the look on
Foley's face. Pure terror. And then surprise and anger, as
Marcus waited to shoot the damned thing until it had raked
its way clear up to Foley's shoulder and was closing in on
his ear.

"What's so goddamn funny?" asked Foley, from across the fire.

"Nothin'," replied Marcus. "Either go to sleep or check to see if that coffee's ready yet. I got no time to talk. I'm thinkin'."

"Fine by me," Foley said, sitting up. "Don't want to talk to you neither, you coward."

"Watch what you say, there, Foley," Marcus barked. "What call do you have to call me a coward, anyway?"

Foley's eyes narrowed. "He was sittin' right there! Right there, Marcus! You coulda plugged him easy. I'm getting tired of this shooting from the trees shit! Makes me feel all crawly in my skin, you know? Like I'm yeller, too!"

Actually Marcus knew exactly how Foley felt, but he wasn't about to admit it.

Frowning, he said, "Get over it or get gone."

"What?"

"You heard me. I'll take care of Slocum in my own damn time. If you don't wanna wait for it, then get goin'. Conversation closed."

Foley stared at him for a long minute, his face torn—as was usual in these moments of confrontation between them—between anger and fear.

And then, instead of answering, Foley simply lay down in his blanket and rolled away, his back to the fire.

And Marcus.

14

Bob Marcus was the brains of the outfit. Foley knew it. But he also new that Marcus was hot tempered and meaner than a chuck-wagon cook.

There was a running joke back in the days when the five of them took turns cooking out on the trail. The joke was one Marcus loved well and told every chance he had:

"Bunch of cowpokes was drivin' cattle when the cook up and died. So the rest of 'em come up with the bright idea to take turns rustlin' up their grub. It *stayed* each person's turn to take a spell over the campfire till someone else was fool enough to complain. Then he'd have to take over. Well, sir, Ol' Tex had been cookin' for two weeks and there'd been lots of grumblin', but nobody'd out-and-out complained. So one night, he added all the chili peppers to the beans, but all he got was some ugly stares. Next night, he tried a handfula dirt. Still nothin'. Finally, outta desperation, Ol' Tex threw in a cowpie. It was more'n one cowboy could stand.

"He said, 'These here beans taste just like cowshit.' Ol'

123

Tex started to get all gleeful-like. Then the other cowpoke quickly added, 'But it's the best damn cowshit I ever et.' "

They'd all got a good laugh out of it, till Cassidy mentioned, "There's a little bit of truth to every joke."

Marcus had never taken a turn over the pots after Cassidy's observation. They'd made sure of it. Tripped over their tongues to complain when it was his turn.

True, they'd had some wind-up, shake-'em-down times together, especially when they'd been tearing up the countryside over by Prescott. Bill Buckley, Abel Cassidy, and Vance Jefferson were the best for thinking up prankish deviltry.

Up until the time they happened upon that Apache woman on the flats past the rock formations called the Dells. They'd sat in the rocks and watched her for a while, grinding corn and patting tortillas out to bake on a hot slab of rock.

Hot damn, she'd been exciting when she took out her tit to feed her baby!

"Come on, gents," Marcus had said. "We'll send smoke signals to the rest of them Apache not to go running off from the reservation."

The five of them had spent the afternoon in her wickiup taking turns with her before it turned ugly. That damn papoose, screaming its brains out in its cradle board. Finally Marcus blew its brains out, right where it hung, just to shut the thing up.

The squaw bitch. She'd fought like a madwoman . . . for a while. Nearly chawed Buckley's nose off, till Marcus knocked her front teeth out and shoved his cock down her throat.

Years later, Marcus still laughed over what he'd done to

her next. And it was still enough to make Foley gag when he thought of it.

To this day he wondered just who the real savage was.

First he'd burned off her hair, then mutilated her face and cut off all her woman parts. Her own mother wouldn't have recognized her. She'd been used up to the point of drawing her last few breaths when he ripped the silver out of her ears and off her neck, and slashed her throat like an antelope's.

The cradle board he threw inside, and set the whole she-bang afire.

Marcus had stuffed his mouth with the tortillas she'd been cooking and said, "There's two good Indians."

They'd had sense to make tracks for town before her buck returned.

That same evening they'd gotten word of the Double Aces payroll. Soon as Marcus heard about that $50,000—all of it in gold—he'd slavered and foamed over the news like a rabid, crazed wolf circling a pool of water.

Money could twist a man's brain—make him do stranger things than when he had dreams of saloon girls after a month on the range. Foley still had nightmares about that squaw—and the folks on the *Butterfield* stage. It wasn't enough for Marcus just to ambush them. He'd gutted the driver and staked the passengers out like hides curing in the hot Arizona sun.

Townspeople thereabouts still believed it was the work of that renegade Apache.

Payback for his woman and baby.

When they'd apprehended that brave's sorry ass, they'd strung him up faster than packrats can funnel down a hole.

Foley had trouble buying that Marcus ever allowed Bill

Buckley to ride off with that gold in the first place. Lord knew, Foley wasn't the smartest post on the fence line, but he was experienced enough to realize it was against Marcus's nature to let Buckley control all that cash.

Something didn't smell right.

Hellfire! Years passed before he and Marcus managed to track Vance down. By then, Buckley was dead and Abel had split off on his own to help his brother with the Bar C. Vance, the slippery bastard, had zigzagged them across the whole New Mexico and Arizona Territories—and then some.

But still, it went against Foley's grain to kill the asshole on a trumped up fight over a bar girl after they caught up with him.

But it wasn't against his partner's grain at all.

Marcus had done a number on Vance before plugging the sniveler. They'd ransacked Vance's saddlebags and pack roll, but other than a few hundred in double eagles and some unusual looking pipestone carvings, there wasn't enough shit in Vance's stuff to give a clue where the rest of the money was squirreled away.

It was someplace back on the Bar C was all he said. But Marcus was positive Cassidy would know right where it was stashed.

Only Cassidy hadn't known donkey shit. In fact, Cassidy had been pushing them to find it faster.

It was Marcus who had the brilliant idea of killing those horses, just to get Cassidy's attention. And he'd made it clear to Cassidy, too—if he didn't ease up pretty damned soon, Miranda would be next.

That's when he'd reminded Cassidy of that Apache woman, and the people on the *Butterfield* stage. But even whipping the blubbering son of a bitch with a pistol hadn't learned them a damn thing.

Marcus had screwed up.

One thing was certain—Foley had found out Marcus was capable of the vilest acts known to man after he'd watched him kill that first mare and her foal. He was wrong thinking he'd never see anything more disgusting than that Apache woman and her baby. Dead wrong. Marcus's words chilled him to the bone—still turned Foley's stomach more than two months later.

As soon as they'd dismounted, Marcus had unbuckled his pants. "First we shoot 'em, then we screw 'em, then we butcher 'em."

"What in Hades are you talkin' about, Marcus?" Foley had asked, shocked to the toes of his boots.

"Soon as I get my dick out, I'll show you."

And that was just what Marcus had done while Foley stood by, puking up last week's enchiladas.

When all this was over—when they'd found the Double Aces gold—he'd kill Marcus himself.

Foley! Nothing but a good for nothing, sanctimonious crybaby, Marcus thought.

He rolled up in his blanket and turned his back to the fire. Foley was good for a few things—sticking his arm into badger holes, rolling a tight quirlie, or boiling water. But he was dumb as a rock. You could piss on his foot and convince him it was rain.

Maybe that was a good thing, too. Good for Marcus, anyway.

But it was glaringly obvious Foley didn't have the heart to be a proper bandit.

Marcus focused his mind on more pressing matters. Right now, Slocum was nosing around, and there was Abel Cassidy to contend with.

Despite all his speed, Slocum would be an easy mark. Marcus had already had him in his sights twice that day. Half the town of Apache Wells either saw or heard that Slocum had laid Foley's cheek open.

And Marcus made sure they knew Foley carried a grudge. A grudge likely to be settled. Cassidy might be harder to explain, but he wasn't the first man to get lost in the desert.

And that left Miranda.

When all was said and done, he'd take over as the new head honcho at the Bar C and she'd be the sweetwater on a dying' man's throat.

Word on his mother's grave.

When all this was over, and they'd found the Double Aces gold, he'd kill Foley himself.

Miranda heard a soft knock on her door. She quickly covered the papers and bag of money, and put her hand in her pocket. Reassuring herself with the derringer, she crossed the room.

"Yes?" she said through the door.

"It is me, Carmelita, señorita." She opened the door and stepped inside. "I have idea. I hope you approve. Berto thinks it's a good idea."

Carmelita! Miranda's grip on the gun relaxed and she withdrew her hand from her pocket. "What do you mean?"

"No matter how you try to explain, this not look good, Miranda. People might think you make up the story about why you kill Señor Abel."

"But the filthy goat tried to rape me!" Miranda shuddered and rubbed her arms.

"You need not try to convince me." Carmelita's gaze dropped to the floor. "Carmelita like to shoot him, too. But not between the eyes. Between his legs! He . . . After your poppy, die, he—" The woman's face was shot through with rage and pain; then she crumpled.

"Don't, Carmelita. I'm sorry." Miranda hugged and bolstered the woman who had been both a second mother and friend to her.

Carmelita straightened her shoulders, wiped her eyes, and continued confidently. "Everyone knows your uncle has been half-crazed over those horses of his. And that he bought the guns of Foley and Marcus to find out who has been doing this despicable deed."

"But, Carmelita, I'm not so sure that pair's telling the truth. Just the opposite. I've had a terrible feeling they might be involved. That they know way more than they let on."

"We find out soon enough, now that Señor Slocum is here." Carmelita shifted from foot to foot. Then she hissed, "I tell Berto not to go for the undertaker. I tell him to bring feed wagon to the back door and drive Señor Cassidy to the canyon where you find those first dead horses. I tell him, dump Señor Cassidy's body for the buzzards and coyotes. That way, when the sheriff find him, he will think your uncle surprise the *bandidos* and gets himself killed."

As Carmelita finished speaking, Miranda heard the wagon, and then two sets of boots pounding across the veranda. The screen slammed and she heard familiar voices in the hall outside her door.

Berto poked his head into the room and asked vehemently, "Carmelita tell you her mind?"

Miranda nodded.

"You listen to her, *si*?" Berto said.

"It seems like the only sensible solution."

Berto nodded approval. "Don't you worry. Berto and Dilly take care of everything. No one's gonna be sorry Abel is gone, or ask too many questions."

Hatred filled the men's eyes.

"Don't take him until morning," Miranda said quietly. "It'll be safer for the men and the horses then."

Dilly stuck his head in, too, and said, "We won't never breathe a word, miss. We're doin' this for all the women on the ranch."

Berto added, "They're gonna sleep a whole lot easier from now on."

Nausea flooded over Miranda. The men didn't need to explain.

Just before the glowing windows of the Bar C came into view, Slocum changed his mind.

He'd lay low the rest of the night and not go back to the ranch.

With Marcus and Foley camped out on the range and Cassidy rampaging around the desert on a wild goose chase, Miranda's safety was assured. He could trust Carmelita to protect her with her life if need be.

With new purpose, he turned Cougar toward Apache Wells. "Time to start investigatin', buddy," Slocum muttered.

Cougar grunted and snorted, then bobbed his head like he understood every word.

Slocum chuckled. "Cougar, old pal? You got more sense than most people I know."

Then he laughed loud and long. "Way more sense than Bob Marcus and his whole damn gang of cutthroats put together."

Before long, they reached Apache Wells and another rip-roaring Saturday night.

15

He settled Cougar into a livery stall himself, since he couldn't find the stableman to save his life. Then he hiked up to the saloon and hotel for a belt and a room. Maybe a little grub, too. He was getting growly in his stomach.

For a Saturday night, Slocum figured the crowd at the bar to be about average. There was a fistfight going on in the corner, a shouting match in progress across the faro table along the opposite wall, and some duded-up card-sharp was about to be run out of town on a rail.

Slocum wasn't acquainted with any of the parties—and there wasn't anyone from the Bar C that he recognized—so he just slid through the crowd and got himself a room and a whiskey.

He carried the whiskey upstairs and let himself into the room, which, thankfully, was at the back of the building, so the sounds of fighting and yelling didn't come up through the floorboards.

Much.

He stomped to the room's single chair, sat down, and

stretched out his legs. He took a drink. He began to think over his plan.

He supposed that somebody ought to clue in the sheriff, although based on what he'd heard from Abel, it wouldn't do much good.

Well, screw Abel, anyway.

He wasn't helping at all, what with his hired guns probably killing the horses in the first place.

He moved to one hip to reach the two double eagles, and brought them out of his pocket. He hadn't examined them closely yet, although he doubted it would do much good.

He was beginning to think that nothing would do much good. Nothing aside from blasting the Bar C and most of its inhabitants into the next life, that was.

He leaned forward, into the lamplight, set his drink on the table, and opened his hand, wherein lay the coins in question.

At first, he could see nothing unusual about them. Two ordinary twenty-dollar gold pieces. But they didn't really look like they'd been out in the weather too long. In fact, they looked like they were fresh from the mint, although the mint mark said "Denver, 1873." The Denver part didn't arouse any suspicions, but the date did.

How did a coin—especially one minted of gold, which wasn't exactly the most durable metal in the world— survive without a scratch for twelve years?

It didn't.

That was all, it just didn't.

Especially after it had lain out, exposed to the Arizona weather—sandstorms and floods, being stomped on by lizards and horses and antelope and who knows what else—for who knows how long.

He stared at the coins a bit longer, then stuffed them back inside his pocket, finished his drink, and headed downstairs again.

This new revelation called for a steak and a beer. Maybe some fried onions, too.

Miranda had recovered—somewhat—from the discovery of the money her father had left behind. Twenty thousand dollars, exactly.

Her skin still buzzing with the thrill of it—and the realization that she could go anywhere, do anything, *be* anything now—she once again turned toward her father's papers.

Carefully moving the last will and testament, which had received most of the blood spatter, she slid more papers out from underneath the stack and carried them to the bed.

There weren't many, and most of them had to do with the ranch. The deed was there, and the land survey report. Her parents' marriage licence, too, and the certificate of Miranda's own birth.

There was a large envelope that contained a pair of pearl earrings and a multi-strand pearl necklace—the ones her mother had worn in the painting in her father's room— and Miranda held them for a long time, tears running down her cheeks, before she put them back and slid the envelope under her pillow.

And then she found something entirely unexpected. It was a letter, addressed to her, from her father.

"My Darling Baby Girl," it began, in his familiar sturdy handwriting.

I guess you aren't such a baby anymore, are you? You'll forgive me for thinking of you that way, I know. If you're reading this, I'm likely dead. And if I died in any sort of mysterious circumstances, as difficult as it may be for you, I think you should look to your uncle Abel as the mischief-maker.

I know how much you love him, honey. But there are things your uncle Abel has done that we kept from you. Bad things. In '73, he disappeared for a time, and we later heard rumors that he'd been involved in a stage robbery up north. They made away with a $50,000 payroll and killed the passengers and driver. It was a nasty business.

When your uncle came back, I confronted him about it. He admitted, finally, that he'd been involved, but said he didn't have the money. Another fellow, a man named Buckley, had the strongest horse and took off with the gold while the others stayed behind to have their "fun." And Abel said that Buckley had hidden the money somewhere on this ranch, to be split up later. Abel swore he didn't know where, and I came to believe him. At least, he spent enough time looking for it.

Always remember that I love you, Baby, and that you were your mama's world. If you haven't found them yet, there should be an envelope in here containing her pearls. They were her mother's, and her mother's before her. Now they're yours. I'm sorry I didn't give them to you earlier, but you were so young when she passed.

All my love, Papa.

Miranda reread the letter three times, then sat there, just holding it. The mere sight of her father's clean handwriting brought fresh tears to her eyes, and the message made it worse.

Granted, it did make her feel better about shooting Abel, but it made her angry, too.

Angry that her father had to cover up for Abel's misdeeds, angry that he'd had to lie to her—and very probably lie to her mama, too.

She wished that he had told her the names of the other men involved, but then, maybe Abel hadn't said who they were. It seemed that Abel hadn't been the most talkative fellow, even back then.

Papa had probably had to beat out of him what information Abel gave.

That made her grin. Her papa could have done it, too.

Probably even Mama. Uncle Abel was a wiry little shrimp, for a man, and she'd always had the feeling that he was a physical coward.

She folded the letter and stuck it under her pillow, right next to the envelope containing her mother's pearls.

A glance at the clock told her that it was nearly eleven. Slocum wasn't coming back tonight, although she wished it more than anything. She had so much to tell him, and she wanted so much to be held in his strong, strong, arms . . .

She put the rest of the papers back on the little table, blew out her lamp, and snuggled down into her covers, her hand on the pearls' envelope.

She dropped off to sleep.

Slocum pulled back his fist and hit the short man right in the nose. The cowboy yelped and blood spurted, and Slocum allowed himself a little grin—until somebody broke a chair across his back!

He whirled and slugged the perpetrator in the stomach, then ducked quickly to avoid another cowhand, brandishing a bottle.

At least it hadn't come to gunplay. Yet. Slocum would surely hate to shoot somebody over an order of fried onions.

But then somebody fired a shot, and the brawling crowd quieted, Slocum included. He looked toward the door to spy the sheriff—or, at least, somebody wearing a sheriff's badge—standing there with a distinctly unamused expression on his face, his arms crossed and his toe tapping.

"All right, goddamn it," the sheriff said. "What was it *this* time?"

The man whose nose Slocum had broken pointed at him and said, "He done got my fried onions!"

The sheriff turned to Slocum. "Well? Did you take his onions?"

The situation was beginning to tickle Slocum, but he managed to keep a straight face. "No, sir," he said. "I only took what was served to me. If this gent was so set on fried onions, I woulda been glad to share. A little."

"Harley!" the sheriff shouted.

A balding head poked out, from the kitchen. "Sir?"

"Harley, you're gettin' the orders mixed up again. Like you do every damned night! Pay attention to what you're doin', man. I'm gettin' sick of cleanin' up your peckerwood messes!"

"That's right, Harley!" added the man with the broken nose. "I was supposed to get fried onions with my steak, too!"

Harley had the good sense to look embarrassed, and said, "Sorry, Calvin. Sorry, Sheriff. Sorry, everybody, I reckon. Come back here and I'll take care of that nose for you, Calvin, don't you worry none."

"Take care'a me, too, while you're at it," Slocum said.

"My dinner got dumped on the floor and trampled during the fracas."

Calvin, holding a napkin to his nose, said, "Sorry, mister."

"No problem. Hope your nose don't hurt too much."

"Been busted before. It'll get busted again, I reckon," Calvin said as he turned away and headed toward the kitchen.

Slocum righted his chair. People sure were touchy in this town.

The sheriff was just leaving as Slocum took his seat, and he called, "Sheriff! Like to have a word with you!"

The sheriff, a tall, thin, middle-aged man with blond hair gone early to gray, and who looked to be all bone and no muscle, sauntered over and stood at the table.

"What is it?" he asked.

Slocum guessed he'd been sound asleep in his chair when somebody reported the brawl at the café. At least, there was crusted sleep at the corner of one eye.

"Care to have a chair?" Slocum asked, and pulled out the one to his right. "I'm a friend of Miranda Cassidy, and I believe they've got some trouble out there that you might want to hear about."

The sheriff's brow furrowed, and he replied, "Yeah, I would."

Before he sat down, though, he yelled, "Harley!" toward the kitchen, and when Harley stuck his head out, he added, "Bring me a piece of that dried apple pie Bertha made this mornin'. With cheese. And a cup of coffee."

Harley nodded, and the sheriff sat down.

He reached in his pocket, pulled out a ready-made and a lucifer, and asked, "What's that old bastard Abel up to this time?"

16

Foley woke with the first light, and stretched to get the kinks out. Eventually, he stood up, then walked to the edge of camp to take a piss.

Marcus still wasn't up when he came back, so he decided to cook up a little of the ham they'd brought along and hadn't needed last night on account of the fresh badger.

He had the pan sizzling and ham browning before Marcus woke up.

"What you doin'?" asked Marcus, sniffing the air. "You cookin' again?"

"Whatcha think?" replied Foley. He wasn't much in the mood to put up with Marcus's taunts this morning.

"Well, don't go burnin' it this time. Nobody likes black ham, 'specially me."

Foley checked the ham again and turned it over. Just in time, too.

"Where's the coffee?" Marcus growled.

"Make it yourself. You're always sayin' as how you can't drink mine."

141

"True enough," Marcus admitted, and filled the pot from his canteen, then added the Arbuckle's. He set it on the fire. "That ham ready yet?"

"Yeah. Get your plate."

Foley forked half the ham onto Marcus's plate, and then started eating the other half out straight from the skillet. He wished the coffee was ready. There was nothing in the world any drier than hot smoked ham in the desert.

"We got company," Marcus said.

Foley twisted to follow his gaze. There, walking slowly up to their hobbled mounts, was a range mare with a filly at her side. Foley heard a suspicious click behind his back, and twisted around to face Marcus again.

Marcus was checking his gun.

"No," Foley said, as firmly as he could muster. "You said we wasn't gonna kill no more horses. You said it wasn't safe no more!"

"I lied," said Marcus, with an ugly grin on his face.

"You put that gun down right now!" shouted Foley with a vehemence that surprised even him.

Marcus cocked his head, like a dog. "What did you just say to me?"

Behind them, Foley's shouts had spooked the mare. He heard her and her filly cantering away. He just kept staring at Marcus, though.

Marcus repeated, "What'd you say, Foley?"

"You heard me."

"You know, my daddy taught me somethin' that's stuck with me my whole life."

Foley's brow creased. What the hell was Marcus talking about now?

"Let me explain," said Marcus. "Now see, there were these warriors, over in Japan. Can't remember what they called 'em. Summer-eyes, maybe. But anyhow, they never took their sword out of its sheath unless they was gonna use it, gonna draw blood with it. Bad luck or somethin'. And I kinda feel that way about my old Smith & Wesson, here. Can't put it away until I use it on somebody or somethin', y'know? It's got to draw blood."

Foley's pulse started drumming in his ears, but he couldn't make himself move. Even if his gun had been anywhere near him, he couldn't have reached for it. He was frozen with fear.

The story was new, but he'd heard that tone in Marcus's voice before.

And it chilled him to the bone every time.

Marcus smiled at him and said, "You always was the worst cook of all time, Foley. And nobody tells me what to do."

With that, Marcus pulled the trigger. Foley didn't even hear the blast, not really.

He just felt something wet on his head, something wet and hot and red seeping down his face, and then he saw no more.

Calmly, Marcus stuck his gun back in its holster before he reached for the coffee.

He poured himself a cup, even though it was barely brewed yet, and took a sip. "Like I said," he intoned, addressing Foley's corpse, "nobody tells me what to do. Or not to do. I hope this here'll teach you a real lesson."

And then he snorted out a laugh.

The coffee was as bad as any that Foley had ever made, and Marcus tossed the contents of his cup out into the weeds.

•　•　•

Having explained—more or less—the situation at the Bar C to the sheriff, who turned out to be named Tom Robertson, Slocum felt a bit better as he rode out to the ranch the next morning. Cougar seemed to be feeling sprightly, too, and traveled with a new spring in his step.

Course, that might have had something to do with those gals from the saloon having been out front when Slocum rode by, and their having made a big fuss over the gelding. "Fancy Pants," they called him, on account of that snowflake blanket on his rump.

As for Slocum, well, they made a big to-do over him, too, but he had Miranda waiting, didn't he?

From what Sheriff Robertson had told him, the horse killings at the Bar C had been duly reported by one Vance Jefferson, a few days before he quit Abel's employ. Now, this struck Slocum as odd, that Abel would send a hand.

If those had been his horses, he would have been up there screaming at the sheriff himself and demanding satisfaction.

But not Abel. He'd sent a hired man.

And one he didn't particularly like, from everything Slocum had found out so far.

Curious.

Slocum rode into the Bar C a different way from any one he'd tried before, and was, to his reckoning, about three miles from the ranch house, when somebody took a shot at him from a far-off ridge.

He wasted no time. He was off Cougar, grabbing his rifle from the boot, slapping Cougar on the rear, and down in the dirt behind a thick clump of bronze-bush in less than half a minute. During which time the sniper shot again.

He missed, but not by much. Slocum heard the sing and

felt the whoosh of air as the bullet sped past his ear, and he swore under his breath.

After checking to see that Cougar had gotten well out of the way—and was likely cantering on to the Colorado River by now—Slocum tried to eyeball the man attempting to kill him. The ridge was far off, but not so far that he didn't catch just a glimpse of a tiny patch of blue moving between two clumps of boulders and weeds along the top.

Hadn't Bob Marcus been wearing a blue shirt last night?

He took careful aim. His training as a sniper during the war hadn't deserted him, but he needed a little bit more of a target than a glimpse of blue, now vanished.

He decided just to take a shot toward the rocks Marcus—or so he thought—had disappeared behind.

He did, and was rewarded almost immediately with returned fire.

He aimed for the place where the shots were coming from, even as the other man's slugs dug up ground at his elbows and his neck, and shattered the brittle bush he was using for cover.

He felt his calf sting sharply, and realized the son of a bitch had hit him in the leg, which only made him madder.

Quickly, Slocum reloaded the rifle and resumed his end of the battle.

This time, it was the other man who felt a slug's sting. Worse than a sting, to hear his gurgling, gasping holler.

A figure in a blue shirt stood up atop the ridge, took a step, faltered, fell. He tumbled clear down the slope, as a matter of fact.

Slocum lay there for a long time, watching, making sure the man wasn't playing possum—and making sure that he'd been alone—before he got to his feet and whistled for Cougar. He just hoped the horse hadn't run clear out of the county.

And he hadn't. A minute or so after Slocum first whistled, Cougar came galloping back from wherever he'd gone, and slid to a stop before Slocum. Slocum patted his neck while the gelding snuffled at the blood streaming a thin course down Slocum's pant leg, and when Slocum tied the wound off with a tourniquet, he had to shove the horse's nose away.

"If you ain't the nursemaidiest horse I ever rode!" he exclaimed, chuckling despite the pain.

At last, he pulled himself up into the saddle once more and headed Cougar toward the downed man. Halfway there, Slocum stuck his rifle in its boot and replaced it with his handgun. He still didn't trust Marcus any farther than he could throw him.

But when he arrived at his destination, he holstered his gun. He immediately saw that Marcus—for it was he—couldn't be anything other than swamp-log dead.

His head was twisted around the wrong way, for one thing.

And for another, he'd been shot right through the neck and his shirt was covered with blood: the sudden gush of blood that Slocum knew was inevitable when a man took such a wound.

He didn't much care to drag the body back to the ranch, although it would have served Marcus right, to his way of thinking. But instead, he set off to round up Marcus's mount.

He found the bay on the opposite side of the ridge—although he couldn't find hide nor hair of Foley, not even a track—and led the horse back to the body. There, he dismounted and managed to heave Marcus's corpse across the saddle and rope it down with Marcus's lariat.

"It's all right, Cougar," he said as he limped back to his horse. "Just another varmint got himself killed, that's all."

He and Cougar slowly led Marcus's horse and Marcus's body back to the ranch.

Miranda came out of the house when she heard Slocum ride in, and was surprised to see him leading a horse—and a body!

"You've been busy," she said after she hugged him hello.

"Couldn't tell you how much," he said, and then suddenly seemed to realize he had need to be concerned. "Where's Abel? And why are you outside the house?"

"We've been busy here, too." She walked around to the other side of the bay he was leading and picked up the body's head by the hair, turning it so that she could see his face.

"My God," she said, although there was no horror, feigned or otherwise, in her tone. "Bob Marcus."

She looked up at Slocum. "Where's his little friend, Foley?"

Slocum shook his head. He wasn't what you'd call handsome, she thought. Not by the standards of the fashionable magazines. But he was certainly good-looking. Ruggedly so. And the best of all men, by far, in bed.

Not that she'd slept with that many of them. But she'd slept with enough to know what a gem Slocum was.

And he was hurt, she suddenly realized.

Her eyes on his calf, she asked, "Is it horrible, Slocum? Your leg, I mean. Do you need me to probe for the slug?"

He grinned at her. "No, baby, I think it'll be all right. Slug went right through."

"Well, get up on the porch and sit down, for heaven's sake," she ordered. "I'll take care of this!"

Grabbing the reins of both horses, she led them toward the barn, shouting, "Berto! Dilly! Are any of you back there?"

From the rocking chair on the porch, Slocum watched while a hand came running out to meet her, and continued to watch while she pointed and gave orders and generally ran the show.

Chuckling, he shook his head. There was no one like Miranda. No one.

At the sound of the front door's creak, he turned to find the Bar C's cook. "Missed you last night, Carmelita, and your good cookin'," he said, grinning. "Almost got shot over an order of fried onions."

But she didn't smile back, and for a moment he wondered if there was something ominous about fried onions in her past.

But she said, "Miss Miranda. Did she tell yet what has happened, Slocum?"

He flicked a quick glance toward the barn. Miranda and the horses had already disappeared into it. He said, "Why? What happened?"

Five minutes later, he wished he hadn't asked.

"What'd they do with the body?"

"Berto, he is to take him to the place of the dead horses this morning. Miss Miranda thought it was best."

"I don't know . . . Jesus! What the hell could Abel have been thinking?"

Carmelita put her hand on his shoulder. "I do not think he was thinking at all, señor. I know he was your friend, but he was like an animal, a wild animal."

"Did Berto take him yet?"

"No. He is still in his bedroom."

Slocum gave a curt nod. "Best tell Berto to leave him there for the time being. We've got a lot of bodies dropping lately, seems like. I've got to think about what to tell the sheriff."

"A lot, señor? Bodies?"

"Tell you later, Carmelita. I don't suppose you could fetch me one of Abel's cigars, could you?"

17

"You did this?" Slocum said to Miranda. They stood in her uncle's bedroom, staring at the body.

"I already confessed, Slocum. I did it with that little derringer of yours." She spoke calmly, as if she were telling him what they were having for supper.

"I did it to save my virtue," she added, somewhat coolly, "and most probably my life as well. In case you're interested."

Slocum nodded slowly. This put everything in a different light.

The plan to take Abel's body and dump it out by the dead horses might have sounded like the perfect setup to Miranda and Carmelita, but it wasn't passing muster with him.

Not by a long shot.

Additionally, they now had a second body—Marcus's—that needed to be explained. Not for the first time in his life, Slocum wondered where in the hell all the witnesses were when you needed them.

He said, "Miranda, call for Berto again."

"Why?"

"I'm sending him into town for Tom Robertson."

Her brows flew up and her jaw dropped, shattering her previous cool and calm demeanor. "The sheriff? Are you crazy?"

"I met your town sheriff last night, Miranda, and he seems like a fairly reasonable man. If your uncle Abel spoke bad of him, well, I'd be disinclined to agree with his assessment."

She stared at the floor for a few seconds before she raised her head and looked into his eyes.

"All right. I'll go with anything you say, Slocum. I'll call for Berto, but then I have something to show you."

"Something . . . good?" he asked, giving her a little squeeze and a wink.

She smiled up at him. "Oh, even better than that."

Slocum sat at the little dressing table in Miranda's room, poring over the papers she'd found in the safe, while Miranda watched from the bed.

It all made sense now. At least, most of it. Abel Cassidy, anyway, and why he was so set on keeping Marcus and Foley on the place. Eighteen seventy-three had been the year of the big stage robbery up by Flag, and everybody knew that the owner of the Double Aces mine—Milton Carmichael, a man for whom Slocum had once done some business—had a bug up his ass about always paying his men with freshly minted coins in gold and silver denominations.

So the letter, the dates of the coins, and half the gang being on the ranch all dovetailed. And so did the horse killings. If Abel had raised sheep, it would have been sheep that were killed. If he'd raised cows, it would have been those. Just so happened that Abel raised horses.

Unfortunately.

Or at least, Abel's brother, Judah, had. Slocum had never met Judah Cassidy, but it sounded, from the tone of his letter and the strength of his business dealings, that he had been on the up-and-up.

It also sounded as if Abel had been nothing but a hired hand all along. At least, his name didn't appear on the deed anywhere.

He'd been riding on his older brother's coattails all along, and even tried to get the ranch for himself by not breathing a word of this arrangement to Miranda.

But still, there should have been other records, duplicates of the will and the survey papers and the mortgage and so on, kept in the bank or the lawyer's office. Duplicates that should have been investigated upon Judah Cassidy's death.

When Slocum asked Miranda about the lawyer who drew up the will and the other legal papers, she said, "Oh, that was old Mr. Clark, poor darlin'. His office burned to the ground about ten years ago, with him in it. The whole town mourned him. He was a nice man, kind of like everybody's grandpa. Always kept peppermints or licorice for the kids, you know?"

Slocum had a few questions about that all too convenient fire, but they could wait until Sheriff Robertson arrived.

A lot of things could, except one.

He stood up from the dressing table, pushing the little chair back as he did, and keeping his balance on the edge of the table.

"Oh, Slocum!" cried Miranda. "How could I forget all about your poor leg!"

"Musta been that I was bein' so brave and all," Slocum said with a straight face.

Miranda grinned up at him. "Get on the bed and get those pants off, Mr. Slocum."

"My pleasure, ma'am," he said as he hobbled over to it, leaning on Miranda. "Boots first, if you don't mind."

Miranda shook her head and said, "You know I do, but I'm going to take pity on the wounded today."

Slocum took off his hat and tossed it, tardily, to the bed poster. "On behalf of the wounded, we are certainly grateful, Miss Cassidy, for this sacrifice on your part."

She put her fists on her hips. "And if you don't stop bein' so damned formal, Slocum, I'm gonna search and probe for that slug till Tuesday with my papa's rusty old Civil War knife!"

"Yes, ma'am!"

She turned her back to him and took one booted foot betwixt her knees, then the other. "I trust you can take care of the pants yourself?" she asked, tossing the last boot across the floor. "I'm gonna go get a fresh basin of water and some clean rags."

By the time she returned, Slocum had not only scrambled out of his britches, but also the rest his clothing. He lay on the bed, belly-side down, with a sheet casually cast over his backside.

Miranda came in, took a look at him—and the expression on his face—and closed the door softly behind her. She smiled. "Slocum, m'darlin', you're in too weakened a condition to be thinkin' about such things."

"Just patch up my cut, Miranda," he said with a chuckle. "I'll be the judge of the other."

Miranda poked and prodded around in his calf until he was ready to holler, and then she suddenly stopped. "Well, you were right. Bullet passed clean through."

"I told you that before," Slocum said through gritted teeth.

"Ah," said Miranda, in a bemused tone that told him she'd remembered all along, the little sadist. "That's right."

"Just bandage it, would you?"

She patted his backside through the sheet. "Now, now, dear. Let's not get testy with your very own Clara Barton."

Slocum gritted his teeth again and turned his face down, into the pillow.

She was infuriating—but not so maddening that he didn't have a gigantic erection hidden between his body and the mattress. It thudded and throbbed with impatience.

At last, he felt a damp cloth against the skin of his calf, dabbing and washing it clean, then the cool of one of the white cotton bandages she'd brought along being wrapped around his calf and shin.

Heaven.

The moment he felt her finish tying off the bandage, he rolled over and took her in his arms. "Now, Miranda," he said.

Smiling coyly, she pushed his hands away, saying, "By my reckoning, we've got at least three, maybe four hours before Berto gets back with the sheriff."

She went to the dressing table and opened a music box, which began to tinkle out a slow version of one of Slocum's favorites since his war days, "Lorena."

Then, swaying from side to side to the plaintive melody, she began to work at the buttons of her bodice.

Berto was, in fact, just riding into town. He went up to the sheriff's office first and, finding not a soul in residence, made himself at home in one of the rockers on the front porch.

Berto had been at the Bar C for years and years. He'd signed on with Miranda's father, liked him very much as a fair man and a good boss, and when Abel had taken over . . . well, by then, he was pretty attached to Carmelita and the little girl.

This whole business bothered him a great deal. It was bad enough about Miss Miranda shooting her uncle. Not that he hadn't deserved shooting, but preferably by another hand. Not Miranda's.

Berto really would have preferred that they dump the body out with the poor slaughtered horses and pretend innocence of the whole matter.

But then Slocum had ridden in with Marcus's corpse. Berto had thought that exceedingly strange. Two bodies in less than twenty-four hours.

And then, on his way into town from the ranch, he had come across a third. Foley. Granger had been his first name, Berto thought. He had ridden out with Marcus last night. Had Slocum killed them both, and only claimed to have shot Marcus? But why?

It was a puzzle.

He was still sitting there, scratching his head, when a loud voice said, "Mornin', Berto! What brings you into town?"

Berto looked up, then stood up, sweeping off his hat. "Sheriff Robertson. I came to see you, actually."

The sheriff opened the jailhouse door. "Well, c'mon in and pull up a chair. Help yourself to the coffee, son."

Once they were both inside and settled, and each had a tin cup of coffee in his hand, Berto started talking. And despite his misgivings, he left nothing out.

The sheriff listened in silence, keenly hanging on every word Berto had to say. And when Berto was finished, he asked a simple question: "What time did Slocum ride in with Marcus's corpse?"

Berto furrowed his brow. "What time? A little before seven, I think. Why?"

The sheriff shrugged. "Any signs of rigor mortis?"

"Huh?"

"Was he stiff as a board?"

The sheriff was making no sense at all, but Berto answered, "No, sir."

"You found Foley on your way in. Was he stiff?"

"Like firewood, Sheriff Robertson."

The sheriff stood up. "Well, let's go pick him up first, then."

18

The sheriff signaled for Berto to stop about twenty yards out from the body and walked up alone, casting his gaze right and left for tracks.

He saw plenty.

Two men had been camped here—Foley and probably Marcus, if Berto was right. They'd had company somewhere during the night, too. Tracks entered the camp from the east, and the rider had stopped for a spell.

Robertson quickly took the visitor off his list—temporarily, anyhow—because he'd ridden out. And Foley's own boot prints crossed on top of the stranger's.

The sheriff followed the prints and found a yellowish stain on the rocks, where Foley had probably taken his morning piss.

That left Marcus as the most likely perpetrator.

But he withheld judgment for a while. He needed more information.

"You see his horse anywhere around?" he called back to Berto.

"No, but I can trail him, if you want," came the reply.

Robertson nodded. "Good. Do that, then. And make sure you're trackin' the right horse!"

Berto said, "It's easy. Foley's horse was shod with a cross bar on the left front. And I should know. I shooed him just last week." He spun his horse and took off toward the south.

Berto was a handy man to have around, Robertson thought. Slowly, he approached the corpse.

Scavengers had already been at the body, but it was recognizable. Granger Foley, shot in the head. Likely hadn't known what hit him. And the shot had come from up close, no more that four or five feet away.

It was looking more like Marcus all the time.

More snooping—as his wife liked to call investigating—turned up a pair of hobbles and all of Foley's tack. His horse had been deliberately set loose, long before Foley had even thought of putting any tack on him.

But the perpetrator hadn't been afraid of being discovered. He'd left Foley in his blankets, made coffee—the pot was still on the dead embers of the fire—then saddled up and ridden out, to the northwest. At a slow jog.

A pretty cool customer, if you asked Robertson.

In no time at all, Berto was back, leading Foley's chestnut gelding.

"That was quick," Robertson said.

Berto shrugged. "He was just out of sight, grazing on some of the good grama grass behind the hill over there. It was the first Mr. Judah brought up from Dragoon Springs."

"I remember," said the sheriff with a nod. "Judah was awful set on improving this place."

"Not like . . ." Berto trailed off.

"No, not like Abel," the sheriff said.

Together, the two men folded Foley's corpse over his horse once it was saddled and tied it down.

"I'm gonna track this other hombre," Robertson said. "Probably the one that did the shooting. You can split off and take Foley back to the Bar C, if you want."

Berto shook his head. "I have a feeling who did this. And a few other things, too. And he is dead. I told you. Slocum killed him."

"Well, that remains to be seen," Robertson said. "I'll do the detecting, and you do the horse-leading."

They mounted up and, with Berto leading Foley's horse, began to follow Marcus's trail.

"Four times!" Miranda said, languidly lying on her back and half off the bed, with her fingers brushing the nap of the rug. "That's a record, Slocum, even for you!"

He grinned around the cigar he'd just lit. "The day's still young," he quipped.

She sat up and faced him. "But I'm not! You're makin' me older by the second, you brigand, you!"

"And I'll still love you when you're a hundred and fifty, Miranda, my girl."

She chuckled. "You'd better!" Then she threw herself on his chest and began nibbling at his chin.

"Whoa up there, gal," Slocum said, laughing. "Four times is my limit. For one morning, anyhow. I'm thinkin' we ought to go see if Carmelita's rustled us up some grub, aren't you?"

She stuck her lower lip out in a pretty pout. "Who needs food when you're here, Slocum? And when I'm rich, to boot!"

He moved her aside and swung his legs over the side of the mattress. "That may be true—I mean, that you can eat all the cash you want now—but this boy needs his lunch!"

He grabbed for his britches and pulled them on, then started a hunt for his shirt.

"Well, in that case," she said, giggling, "I suppose we should eat something."

"Besides," he added, tossing her petticoat toward the bed, "the sheriff's due pretty soon."

"Oh, phooey."

"It was here," the sheriff said, dismounting.

Berto saw the traces immediately. They were high atop a ridge. The grass and brush behind the boulders that dotted its edge had been beaten down by quick bootsteps in some places. In, others, by the full length of a man's body. Marcus had left his horse below, then traveled up the ridge on foot to ambush Slocum.

He saw, too, a large gush of blood, still damp enough to be drawing flies, just at the side of one of the boulders. He'd seen Marcus's body, and immediately knew this was where Marcus had received the killing shot.

As if reading Berto's mind, Sheriff Robertson said, "Yeah, he fell here," and pointed down the steep side of the ridge. He stared. "Went bucket over barrel, too."

He turned back to where Berto sat on his horse and held Foley's. "Reckon Slocum told you the truth, all right. I can see his tracks down there, at the bottom and out a ways. He got himself ambushed, pure and simple."

Berto allowed himself a small sigh of relief. He liked to think he knew an honest man when he met one, and Slocum—despite all those dime books, of which Berto had read a few—seemed honest.

He was glad the sheriff had seen what he'd seen, and said what he'd said.

"Back to the ranch, now?" Berto asked. He glanced up

at the sun. "If we hurry, we might be in time for one of Carmelita's good meals."

The sheriff swung up on his buckskin. "Sounds like a heckuva good plan to me, Berto. Lead on."

Slocum and Miranda were just sitting down to a grand noontime spread—roast pork in plum sauce, candied yams, fried potatoes, peas, and applesauce—when Carmelita answered a knock at the door.

Behind him, Slocum heard, "Ah, Sheriff Robertson! Come in, come in! You too, Berto! I am just serving lunch if you would care to—?"

"Join us?" Miranda broke in, rising. Robertson's face lit up like Christmas. It was obvious he'd had a taste of Carmelita's cooking before. Miranda ran to help with the extra plates.

Slocum stood up, too, and shook hands with both men. "Good timing, Robertson," he said with a grin, and motioned to two empty chairs. "You, too, Berto. Have a seat!"

When both men were seated and served and had gotten past the first heady bites of Carmelita's cooking, Robertson said, "Well, we've got a little surprise for you, Slocum."

"What's that?"

"We found Foley's body out there. Well, actually, Berto here, found it on his way into town, and bird-dogged me back to it on the way out here."

Slocum frowned. "What happened to him?"

"Well, looked a whole lot like your pal Marcus did him in."

"I'll be damned!" Slocum said. "Marcus killed Foley?"

"And we found the place where you killed Marcus," Robertson went on, and helped himself to another slice of pork. "Everything was just like you said." He scooped extra plum sauce on it and continued, "So I wouldn't worry none about an inquest or a trial. I'm satisfied, and if I am, the circuit judge is gonna be, too."

Slocum nodded his gratitude. He had to. His mouth was full of yams.

"I imagine we can put off Abel till after dinner?" said the sheriff.

"Please do," Miranda said distastefully, and put her fork down and her hands in her lap.

"Miss Miranda?" said Carmelita from the kitchen doorway, "You no like what I fix?"

"Yes, I do. Sorry, Carmelita. Just thinking about Uncle Abel again . . ."

Carmelita addressed all the men in the room when she shook her finger and said, "Shame on you! Shame on you for upsetting my Miss Miranda!"

She went to Miranda's chair, helped her up, then walked her down the hall, murmuring to her the whole time.

"Sorry," said Berto, automatically.

"You didn't have nothin' to do with it," Robertson said, cutting his meat. "It was my big mouth. Hope she don't get the vapors . . ."

Slocum figured there was little chance of that, but said nothing. In fact, he was waiting for Robertson to ask him his side of the story. Any story. There were so many to choose from!

But he held his tongue. Or rather, he kept it tied up in Carmelita's good lunch. The sheriff and Berto beat him to the finish, though. Robertson pushed back from the table and loosened his belt a couple of notches, and Berto belched loudly before excusing himself.

"Just a warnin', Sheriff," Slocum said. "If you don't

want to get your ass kicked from here to kingdom come by a couple of women, you'll take off your spurs."

Robertson suddenly looked guilty. "Thanks," he said, reaching down to unbuckle the first one. "Forgot. Carmelita's hell on wheels about that."

"Miranda, too."

"Reckon so, by this time. Hell, I ain't been out here in years! Eight or nine of 'em, maybe. Abel didn't like company."

"For good reason," Slocum said.

Robertson lifted his brows. "And that'd be?"

Well, he was in for it now. Slocum worked his jaw muscles once or twice, then he said, "For one thing, it's my opinion that he killed his own brother."

Surprisingly, he got no argument from Robertson. Instead, the sheriff simply sat there and nodded. "Wondered about that, myself. Wasn't anything anybody could prove, though."

"A motive?" asked Slocum.

"None I knew of."

"Tell me somethin'. Did Judah Cassidy die before or after lawyer Clark's office burned down?"

Robertson looked totally lost. "Gomer Clark? How'd you know anything about Gomer Clark?"

"Miranda. Plus which, I read the original will. The copy got burned up in the fire, I guess."

"Yeah, it did. Most of the town's legal papers went up that day."

"Well, I got a feelin' that Abel Cassidy had a hand in it. Can't prove a damned thing. But Judah left this ranch to Miranda, not Abel. Abel never did own one part of it. Just worked here as a hired hand."

The sheriff's jaw dropped. Slocum took advantage of

the lull in the conversation to go fetch himself a cigar. He brought back one for Robertson, too.

After Robertson accepted the cigar, he said, "Can I see this will?"

"Don't see why not. Think there are a few other papers you might want to have a gander at while you're at it, too."

"Fair enough," Robertson said, and bit the end off his cigar. "This is turnin' out to be a very interestin' day."

19

At last, Tom Robertson looked up from the stack of papers he'd been going over for the last hour.

"You were right, Slocum," he said. "Abel was tryin' to pull off some mighty funny business, and he just about got away with it, too. Sorry, Miss Miranda. Sorry about . . . everything."

He lowered his eyes then, and Miranda muttered, "It's all right, Tom. It wasn't your fault, none of it. And now it looks like we've got some treasure hunting to do, once everyone's . . . up to it."

He nodded, then looked over at Slocum. "You gonna stick around and help?"

"Thought I would," Slocum replied. "Course those boys've been lookin' a real long time, and they didn't come up with anything. I'm wonderin' if Vance Jefferson didn't find it and take off with it. It doesn't sound like somethin' Vance'd do, but then, neither does robbin' a stage."

Robertson nodded. "I agree. I liked him. Seemed on the up-and-up when I knew him."

"There any reward for that gold, Sheriff?" Slocum asked.

"Oh, I reckon there is," Robertson said, setting the papers aside. "Have to check. Send a few telegrams, maybe write some letters, that sorta thing. I don't even know if the Double Aces is still producin', or if the owner, what's his name—"

"Milton Carmichael." Slocum broke in. "Grand old feller."

"Right," said the sheriff with a nod that said he didn't have the slightest idea what Slocum was talking about. "Don't know if Mr. Carmichael is even alive, or if he has any heirs. That robbery was a long time back, and I hear that Carmichael was old even then."

"Twelve years ago," said Slocum.

"Isn't there a statue of limits or something?" Miranda piped up.

"A *statute* of limitations," Slocum said, his mouth twitching into a grin.

"Yes'm," Robertson said with a straight face. "But to be fair, I'd sure like to see if anybody wants to lay claim to it. I mean, you don't have to make the offer, Miranda, God knows. But what with you havin' the ranch and that bag a cash your papa left you, don't seem to me like you're in dire need."

"True," said Miranda.

She looked mighty disappointed, but Slocum saw the sheriff's point. And Milton Carmichael's, if he was still alive. He'd been close to eighty when Slocum worked for him, and that was a few years before the robbery.

There might be kin, though, and they might really need some cash.

Berto and Dilly were just carrying out Abel's sheeted corpse on an old door, and Robertson glanced at it.

He said, "No need to haul him into town. Go ahead and plant him, boys. I'm satisfied that the case is closed."

"Don't put that . . . Don't put him anywhere near my daddy or mama," Miranda said.

Berto nodded his understanding. "The other side of the hill," he said, and Carmelita stepped quickly to open the door for them.

Slocum overheard Carmelita whisper, "Will you bury them tonight?"

"Yeah," replied Berto.

"Mark it," said Carmelita, "so I can spit on his grave. Mark it with the sign of the devil. Mark them all that way, all three of them."

Berto nodded, and the men—and their burden—moved through the door. Carmelita closed it behind them, then leaned against it and made the sign of the cross, her eyes closed as if everything was finally settled and she could only just now take the time to pray.

"The sign of the devil, Carmelita?" Slocum asked, interrupting her.

"The upside-down crucifix, señor," she said as she straightened. There was a grand sort of conviction in her voice. "So that Our Lord and Savior will close the gates of Salvation to them."

Then she walked away, into the kitchen. "Enchiladas again tonight," she called back, over her shoulder, in a voice that showed no enthusiasm whatsoever. Except perhaps to take out some more of her frustration on Abel's corpse.

"Whatever," answered Miranda, who didn't seem to notice. "Whatever you can throw together."

"Sky's clear," said Robertson, hopefully. "Likely, it'll stay that way till after sunset."

"Yes, Tom, you're invited to stay," Miranda said. "But won't your missus worry?"

"No, I told Deputy Riley to wait an hour, then to go and

tell her I was ridin' out this way." He smiled ruefully. "Knowin' her, she would have come along, too, just for a taste of Carmelita's cookin'."

"Next time," Miranda said most graciously, Slocum thought, for someone who'd just been asked if her privacy could be invaded. "When things are more . . . normal. I haven't seen Priscilla in ages, and I'd be glad for her company."

"Thanks!" said the oblivious sheriff. "I'll pass along the invite!"

"I thought he'd never leave," said Miranda as she pulled off Slocum's second boot.

"Put a kink in your afternoon?" Slocum asked, grinning.

"You smart-ass," she said, shaking a finger. Her breasts jiggled along with it. She was nude. "It put a kink on yours, too! And most of your evening! Why'd you have to offer him brandy and a cigar?"

"Because he's a nice fella. Because I like him. And at least we know everything's legal now," Slocum said, and belched loudly.

Miranda shook her head. "Men. They shouldn't be allowed to live in the house."

"Hand me my boots, then, and I'll head out to the barn. There's an empty stall next to Cougar's that looked mighty cozy," he said teasingly.

Miranda laughed and climbed atop him on the bed, straddling him. She took both his hands and placed them on her breasts. While he gently kneaded and fondled them, she purred, "And just when did you get to be so sensitive to my every whim, Slocum?"

He gave one nipple a tweak and she hissed in air. "No fair!"

He cocked a brow. "No fair?"

"You don't have your britches off yet, darlin'," she whispered.

He laughed, and while he did, she pulled his britches off with a whoosh, like a magic trick. They made love slowly and leisurely until far into the night, and fell asleep in each other's arms.

When morning dawned, Slocum and Miranda enjoyed a good breakfast—without Carmelita, who Slocum guessed was probably out spitting up a storm in the graveyard—then saddled their horses.

"Do we have to go on this fool's errand today?" Miranda had whined over her eggs. "I thought maybe we could have one day just to stay in bed!"

Slocum grinned at her.

"It's only a fool's errand if it doesn't pay off, honey," he'd said cryptically, and then let it go at that.

She hadn't had any ammunition to come back at him with.

And he really thought he knew where to look for that gold. At least, he was pretty sure that he did. He figured Miranda's daddy had a good idea where it was, too, and maybe had sampled just a tad of that gold before his brother killed him.

A lot of people had died for that payroll money, and Slocum wasn't going to rest until he figured it out and saw it come to an end, whatever that end might turn out to be.

On the ride out, they passed a crew of Miranda's men, whom Slocum had instructed to go throw some dirt—and rocks—over what was left of the horse carcasses. He hoped it would keep the coyotes at bay, anyhow.

All the men seemed to look to him to give the orders now. He figured they were relieved. Abel hadn't seemed to care one way or the other about anything except profit and playing faro, but the men were glad to do some good work for a change.

Their buckboard contained not only picks and shovels, but what looked to Slocum like kerosene. They were going to make a finish to it, then. He approved.

Besides, the men had a small herd of horses coming in from the range in a few days, horses they were supposed to top off for the cavalry. This filled in the downtime.

"Where are we headed, Detective Slocum?" Miranda asked, with a chuckle in her voice.

"Out to our little waterfall and pool," he replied, smiling.

"Aha!" she cried, with an impish grin. "Well, it's sort of like our second bedroom . . ."

"Not so fast, Lady Godiva," he said. "Don't go haulin' out the soap or rippin' those clothes off quite yet. We're gonna do us a little prospectin'."

"Oh," Miranda said, dejected. "With picks and sledge-hammers and dynamite? Why do I have the feeling I'm not going to have any fun?"

"No picks, no sledgehammers, and especially no dyna-mite, I promise," he said. "And you'll have yourself some fun, all right, Miranda my girl. At least, I'm hopin' you will!"

"I will?"

"Yes, you will," he promised. "Now gig that fancy quarter-mile runnin' horse of yours into a canter, and let's get there!"

Once again, they climbed the cliff to the pipestone quarry, Miranda sidling along the rock face behind Slocum. There was no way he'd trust those little mocassin footholds to get him up the slope, so they took their original path, the old one that Miranda had been climbing since she was a kid.

This time, however, Slocum carried his saddlebags over his shoulder. Inside, he had candles, lucifers, a couple of small rock hammers, and the chunks of pipestone Miranda had found in the safe.

He was putting a lot of faith into his instincts, which had always served him well in the past. He hoped they wouldn't desert him now.

At last, he squeezed himself into the crescent opening of the little cave, then helped Miranda in behind him.

"Is this—" she began, but he cut her off with a wave of his hand.

"Just hush and hold your horses a second," he said, as he sat down and opened his saddlebags.

He lit the first candle and handed it to her. "Find someplace to perch that," he said, while he lit another. In a few moments, the cave was bright with the light of a dozen candles, all Slocum had managed to scrounge from the house.

"Why, it's beautiful," Miranda whispered.

It was, indeed. The flickering candlelight brought out the red and white striations in the rocks, made the uneven, crudely mined walls seem pretty, and plainly showed where the fingers of pipestone began and ended, and where the surrounding rock took over.

Next, Slocum pulled the pipestone pieces from his saddlebags. He handed half to Miranda.

"How are you at puzzles?" he asked.

"I'm a wizard at jigsaws, if that's the kind of puzzle you mean," she replied, looking at him quizzically.

"Exactly the kind," he said. "I want you to see if you can figure out just where those came from."

"These rocks? Are you crazy?"

"Maybe," he said, and went to work trying to match up the other half.

• • •

Tom Robertson had been busy.

He had established that the Double Aces mine had in fact played out and closed down more the seven years ago, and that Milton Carmichael, landowner and mining magnate, had died soon thereafter.

"Hope you didn't leave no heirs, Milton," he muttered to himself as he wrote a few more telegrams. "Apache Wells could use a big influx of cash."

After he finished writing a second wire to Milton Carmichael's lawyers and one to a friend in the U.S. marshal's office up in Prescott, he strolled down to the telegrapher's office and handed them to the clerk.

"Somethin' big happenin', Tom?" asked Harry, Apache Wells's telegrapher.

Tom Robertson kept a stoic face. "Could be, Harry, could be. How's that boy of yours?"

"Bill!" Harry exclaimed, his attention diverted from the contents of the telegrams in his hands. "Oh, he's fine. Gonna play first base for the town team this year. Got an arm on him, that boy has. Takes after his pop," he added, proudly.

Robertson smiled. "Good, good. Just send the wires, Harry."

"Oh! Right away!"

And when Harry had finished his rat-a-tat-tatting, Robertson held out his hand again. "Originals?"

Harry handed them back. "Must be pretty big doin's, all right! I'll send a runner when the replies come in, okay?"

"Good enough," replied the sheriff. "Thanks, Harry!"

20

Slocum was about to give up.

He had explored every inch of the little cave, reached back into every cubbyhole, tried his stones against every inch that even halfway looked like it might match, and still nothing.

Nothing!

Miranda had thrown in the towel about ten minutes earlier. She sat dejectedly in the opening, facing out, kicking her bootheels rhythmically against the hillside, like an obstreperous child.

Well, he guessed he'd been wrong, and he guessed he couldn't blame her. He wished she'd quit drumming those heels, though!

He blew out the candles, tossed the pipestone chips back in his saddlebags, and made for the opening. "Look out, honey, I'm comin' through," he said. Maybe he'd work off a little of his frustration with Miranda down in that pool, after all.

She twisted and started down the hill, using the ancient

hand- and footholds, and he figured what the hell. He'd go that way, too.

Even if he ended up slipping and sliding down on his belly, at least it'd be faster.

But after only two steps down the sheer hillside, he lost his foothold and grabbed quickly for the only thing in sight, which was a chunk of half-dead brush sticking out of the hill.

Unfortunately, it gave way and pulled out, roots and all, at the mere pressure of his hand.

But fortunately, something else came loose with the roots.

Tangled in them was a small metal box, which tumbled out, nearly fell on Slocum's head, and bounced to the bottom of the rise, cracking open when it hit the hard sandstone floor and spilling forth a sparkling treasure trove of golden and silver coins.

"Holy shi—" cried Slocum as he slid down the face of the hill, right behind the box.

He knocked Miranda off her moorings on his way down, and she fell right behind him, screaming, "Slocum! You're a—"

They hit the bottom, and she landed on top of him. "A genius!" she finished, and clambered off him to go count her prize.

Slocum sat up a bit more slowly, rubbing the back of his neck. He slid his hips to one side, to get off the rock he'd landed on, then rubbed his ass.

That's gonna leave one helluva bruise, he thought angrily, and then remembered the money. His scowl turned to a grin right away and he stood up and walked the two steps to where Miranda sat, happily running the glittering, clean-as-the-day-they-were-minted coins through her fingers.

"Oh, aren't they just beautiful, Slocum?" she chirped. "Aren't they glorious?"

He didn't think he could have scrubbed that grin off her face with a wire brush, even if he had wanted to.

He sank down on his heels next to her and picked up the empty cashbox. The lock was broken off, but it otherwise seemed usable.

"Let's get it all back inside," he prompted gently.

She pouted fetchingly. "Oh, Slocum!"

"Now, Mandy . . ."

"Oh, all right."

She began scooping up coins and placing them in the box while Slocum picked up the broken lock. He looked at it, scowled, then held it closer.

Rust. There was rust on the broken lock, on the pieces that joined it and had ostensibly just broken open.

Curious.

But then again, not so curious. Jefferson would have had to bust that lock open to get some coinage out. But why the hell hadn't he taken more? There was a whole lot left.

Slocum shrugged and said nothing. It was none of his business. Likely, Carmichael's heirs would be too busy fighting over what was left to notice a few missing hundred.

He began to scoop half the coins into his saddlebags, and Miranda said, "Hey! What the hell are you doing?"

He chuckled a little before he said, "What d'you think, Mandy? That I was gonna load up, then hit the trail to Mexico?"

She snorted softly. "Well, no, not exactly."

"I'm splitting the load up, that's all. This stuff is heavy."

"Oh," she said, and appeared to relax. "Right. And then what are we going to do with it?"

"Take it into town."

Again, she appeared dejected, but then brightened a little. "Well, we promised, didn't we?"

"Yup," said Slocum, still scooping up coins. There seemed to be millions of them! Well, thousands, anyway. "We did."

The stench of burning horseflesh was beginning to reach Slocum's nose. The boys must have decided to burn some of the carcasses before they covered them up.

He scooped up the last of the coins, stood up, then hoisted the heavy saddlebags over his shoulder.

He whistled for Cougar, and Miranda's mount followed the Appaloosa up.

"Sorry about the weight, boy," he said to Cougar as he settled the bags up behind the saddle and secured them. He opened Miranda's saddlebags and poured half the contents of the chest into each side.

"Leg up?" he asked her.

She nodded, and he gave her a boost up into her saddle, then mounted Cougar, still holding the empty strongbox under his arm.

"What are you taking that old thing for?" Miranda asked as they set off for town.

Slocum shrugged. "Evidence?"

"Can we get something to eat before we go to the sheriff's office?" asked Miranda when they finally rode into town. She had made it plain, during the long ride into Apache Wells, that she was turning the money in only under duress.

"No," replied Slocum. His pattern of answers to her had turned monosyllabic.

"But—"

"No."

He rode straight to the sheriff's office, with Miranda trailing behind, tied Cougar to the rail, then waited for Miranda to catch up.

She was taking her own sweet time, but at least she was coming. Slocum had to give her that. After all, she was under no legal obligation to return the cash, and all that gold right under one's nose was one hell of an inspiration to just take off with it.

He'd have to cut her a little more slack, he decided as he helped her down from the saddle.

He picked up the empty cashbox again, took Miranda's arm, and proceeded through the open office door.

Robertson was dozing at his desk, but woke at the sound of Slocum's bootsteps.

He took one look at the cashbox under Slocum's arm and cried, "You found it!"

Rounding the desk in nothing flat, he grabbed the box away. Then noticing that it was far too light, he said, "You didn't find it?"

Slocum said, "It's outside, divvied up in the saddlebags. Brought the box in, though. Lock's been shot through, and a long time back, I reckon, from the rust."

Robertson squinted at the lock. "You're right." He looked up again. "How much was left?"

"Don't know."

Miranda crossed her arms and added, "He wouldn't let me take the time to count it."

"Reckon they can do that at the bank," Robertson said, and led the way outside. "What say we drop off this treasure of yours and then go down to Harley's and have a bite to eat?"

"Fine by me," Slocum said, and Miranda nodded agreeably.

Over barbecue, Sheriff Robertson told then what he'd discovered—that Carmichael was dead and the mine was closed. He was waiting for more information about the heirs.

If there were any, that was.

Slocum grunted—he had figured as much—but Miranda seemed thrilled at the news.

"I wonder what they're up to . . . ," she said.

"Who?" Slocum and Robertson asked, as one.

"The bank, you sillies," she said, shaking her head. "You know, those coin-counter people! I wonder how much they're up to."

Slocum just shook his head, but Robertson looked over at her and grinned.

It wasn't that Slocum didn't understand their excitement over all that cash. It was just that he considered it a tad premature, that was all.

Just as they were pushing their chairs away from the table, a kid came in. The sheriff recognized him and shouted, "Hey, Georgie! Lookin' for me?"

The boy grinned and headed over to the table, then handed Robertson two telegrams. "There you go, Sheriff," he said. Robertson dug into his pocket, but when it didn't look like he was coming up with anything, Slocum flipped the kid a quarter.

"Thanks, mister!" the boy said, wide-eyed, and scampered out.

"You're too generous, Slocum," Miranda reprimanded him.

"For good luck," he said with a shrug.

They both stared at Robertson, who was reading the telegrams.

He looked up abruptly, folding the papers and sticking them in his pocket. "Let's go up to the bank, see how they're comin'."

Slocum's brow furrowed, but it was Miranda who asked, "Hey! What's the news, Sheriff? You can't just get a fistful of telegrams—which probably have to do with us—and not say a word about them!"

"Miranda," he said, "my lips are sealed for the time being."

As she stomped out of the café in Robertson's wake, Slocum heard her mutter, "Damn!"

At the bank, three tellers were seated in the manager's office counting the coins into piles of ten. They were nearly finished, and so Miranda, Slocum, and the sheriff stood quietly in a corner and let nature take its course.

Well, actually, Miranda started to say something, but Slocum pinched her backside, distracting her.

At last, the teller marking the tally sheet said, "All right. Mr. Meyers?" The bank president, a portly fellow in a three-piece suit, who had been seated in a corner chair and unnoticed by Slocum or the others, stood up, startling Miranda.

"Yes, Quimby?" said Meyers.

Quimby handed over the tally sheet; then he and the other bank employees left the room and closed the door behind them.

Meyers took his seat behind the desk. His eyes zigged back and forth and he read the numbers, and then he looked up.

"Miss Cassidy," he said, in a proper banker's tone, "Sheriff Robertson has explained your situation. Please know that you can count on us to be of any possible assistance."

"How much is left?" Slocum asked, before Miranda could.

Meyers raised his brows. "And who are you, sir? Are you somehow involved in this matter?"

"Mr. Meyers," said the sheriff, "this here's Slocum. He's the one responsible for findin' the gold in the first place."

Meyers nodded. "Well, my congratulations to you, Mr. Slocum. Do I take it that the reward will go to you, then?"

"No sir," Slocum said quickly. "It was found on Cassidy land. Oh, and these two, too!" He dug into his pocket and brought out the two gold pieces he'd found by the stream, and placed them on the desk.

"Well, then," said Meyers. "Now that that's straightened out . . ." He consulted his pad again, added forty dollars to the total, and pronounced, "There is exactly $46,540 dollars. To the penny." He looked up at the sheriff. "I trust you wish this put into our safe depository for the time being?"

"Jefferson sure didn't take much," Slocum muttered.

Meyers, who hadn't heard the comment, said, "Well?"

Sheriff Robertson stepped forward. "I think that's up to Miss Cassidy here."

Miranda could hardly contain herself. "Me? Up to me?"

Robertson grinned. "There aren't any heirs, Miranda. I just heard from Carmichael's lawyers. Seems he left the whole of his estate to the Territory of Arizona, and you're not obligated to hand over a penny of it. It's all yours."

Slocum caught Miranda just before she collapsed to the floor.

21

After Slocum carried the unconscious Miranda up to the hotel and got her settled and comfortable, he took himself a walk back up to Tom Robertson's office. The windows still glowed, and he walked right in.

"She's still out like a light," he said as he poured himself a cup of coffee.

Robertson nodded. "Probably best to just let her stay in town tonight. She's been through an awful lot for such a tiny person. What is she, anyhow, five-foot-nothin'?"

Slocum nodded his agreement, and pulled out his fixings bag in preparation to roll a quirlie. "Five-one, I think."

Robertson stopped him with a wave of his hand. "Try one of these," he said, holding out a box of real, honest-to-God Havanas.

"If I'da known you were such a connoisseur, I woulda stopped in a lot earlier, Tom," Slocum said, gratefully accepting a cigar. "Sorry about that shitty cigar I offered you last night. Abel Cassidy never had much taste in smokes, I guess."

"By the by," Robertson said as Slocum bit off the end of his cigar and lit it, "you've got a good friend in Templar Bond."

"Templar?" Slocum asked, not making the connection. Well, he knew who Templar was, but he couldn't figure Robertson into the equation.

"Up at Prescott," Robertson explained as he lit his own. "In the U.S. marshal's office. Seems to think right highly of you."

Slocum just said, "Huh?"

"Oh, I been busy today, Slocum. Been firin' off wires right and left."

"And you wired the U.S. marshal's office? About the gold, or about me?"

Robertson sniffed. "You, naturally. I got paper on you. Old paper, granted. But I wanted to make certain I didn't have another scofflaw or brigand on my hands."

Slocum smiled. "And Templar spoke up for me." It wasn't a question.

"That he did," Robertson said. "Offered you a job while he was at it."

"Wire him back that the answer's still no."

Robertson nodded. "I guessed that he'd been after you for quite a while. After you in a good sense, that is."

This time, Slocum grinned. "That he has. You know, this is a damn fine cigar. I hear those Cuban girls roll 'em on their bare thighs. Calls for stronger stuff than coffee to go with it, I figure."

"Thought you'd never suggest it, Slocum," said Robertson, with a twinkle in his eye. He stood up, shutting an open desk drawer with his leg. "I suggest that we adjourn to the saloon."

Slocum stood up, too. "I'd say that was a right fine suggestion."

Carmelita's grandmother had been a *bruja,* a Mexican witch of sorts, and Carmelita had grown up listening to her cast spells and curse fields and help those in troubled and difficult childbirth.

She had grown up in a small *casita* thick with the scents of drying herbs, pigeon hearts, and chicken's feet, and the sounds of mumbled prayers and chants. Charms hung in the windows and on the doors, and had been sold to villagers to stop a straying husband or cure a fruitless womb, or help the stock gain strength and stay free from disease.

Magic had been everywhere.

After a day spent principally in calling upon her grandmother's spirit to help with the devising of some very satisfying curses to cast over the dead men's graves, Carmelita stood on the porch.

The setting sun was at her back and her fingers absently worked a dishrag while she watched the men slowly come in with the buckboard.

Berto hopped down on the way past and greeted her, taking off his hat. "It's a fine evening, Carmelita."

"Good evening, Berto," she replied. "Is it all taken care of? The horses, I mean?"

"Yes," he said with a curt nod. "We burned what we could, and buried what was left. There will be no more killings now, thank God."

He paused and thumbed back his hat. "I hope Slocum will stay, Carmelita. I hope he will marry our Miss Miranda. He is one hombre I would be proud to work for."

Carmelita shook her head. "That is my wish, too, but I

don't think it is to be. Miss Miranda, she says he has the itching feet. I don't know what this is, but she says it means he is always wanting to be someplace else, someplace he isn't." She shrugged. "I do not understand."

"I've heard of men like that," Berto answered. "Sometimes, they call them saddle tramps."

Carmelita shot him one of her nastier looks, but he wasn't watching.

"And sometimes they call them knights in shining armor," he added. "Gallant men."

"I like that defining better," she said.

Berto nodded. "So do I."

He moved on, and once again, she thanked her lucky stars that her grandmother had been a powerful *bruja,* to give her the power to forever curse those men to hell.

Miranda woke on cool sheets, behind drawn drapes, and it took her a second to get her bearings. She was at the hotel, she decided. And Slocum must have brought her here.

"And I'm rich, too!" burst from her lips.

She heard Slocum's chuckle coming from the far corner of the room, then his baritone rumble. "Yes, darlin', that you surely are."

He stood up in the shadows and came closer, until she could see him.

"How's it feel?" he asked, grinning.

She sighed gleefully. "Wonderful. Absolutely wonderful. Fantastically, *magnificently* wonderful!"

"And that's just how it should feel."

She pushed herself up into a sit and held out her hand to him. "Oh, Slocum, I'm so happy, but I feel . . . guilty, too."

"About?"

"Uncle Abel. He had his good moments, too," she said.

"He used to take me fishing after Papa died. And he helped me train Sundancer. All kinds of things, big things and small things you wouldn't think to mention. I don't understand . . . I mean, I just don't . . . Right after I killed him, I felt so justified, you know? But now . . ."

She began to cry—for a lost childhood, for all the lies she'd believed, for everything. And then Slocum's broad arms came around her, filling her with hope for the future and faith in people.

And with need.

"Abel was a bad man, darlin'. He killed your papa, and others, too, and tried to cheat you out of your ranch. Your birthright. A few good deeds don't change that, not a bit," he whispered.

He was right, and she knew it with all her heart. She looked up at him, blinking away the tears. "Why'd you do it?"

His expression turned quizzical. "Do what?" he asked.

She said, "Put those two gold pieces back. They were yours. I gave them to you."

He smiled at her, and brushed away a new tear with his thumb.

"Didn't know it was yours to give me at the time." He shrugged slightly. "Figured what with you givin' up so much, the least I could do was pitch in forty bucks."

She grinned up at him. "You're getting it back, you know."

He returned the grin. "Rather take it out in trade, you little minx, you."

She giggled and kissed him.